BEST MICROFICTION

2020

Series Editors
Meg Pokrass, Gary Fincke

Guest Editor
Michael Martone

BEST MICROFICTION 2020
ISBN: 978-1-949790-30-6

First Pelekinesis Printing 2020

For information:

Pelekinesis
112 Harvard Ave #65
Claremont, CA 91711 USA

ISSN 2641-9750

www.pelekinesis.com

Best
Microfiction
2020

Best Microfiction Anthology Series

Series Editors
Meg Pokrass, Gary Fincke

Guest Editor
Michael Martone

Contributing Editor, North America
Bill Cook

Contributing Editor, UK, Europe, Australasia
Frances Gapper

Copy Editor
Michelle Christophorou

Project Support
Sherry Morris

Layout and Design
Mark Givens

Cover illustration
Terry M. Givens

TABLE OF CONTENTS

BEST MICROFICTION

THREE ESSAYS ON CRAFT

WHAT THE EDITORS SAY: INTERVIEWS WITH THE YEAR'S TOP MICROFICTION MAGAZINES

FOREWORD

MEG POKRASS AND GARY FINCKE,
SERIES CO-EDITORS

The more I become involved in the editorial side of the microfiction form, the more it becomes mysterious to me. After reading thousands of stories for *Best Microfiction*, all I can say is that there is no formula. The other thing I can say is that we must use who we are when we write. Trying to perfect a "style" is useless. Making something that feels like you, something only you can possibly see that way, works wonders. The secret seems to be in revealing who you are through the life of a character or two, which somehow mysteriously makes us see something unusual about the world itself. Finding your own expression of something we all have felt before, in some sly and startling way that hooks us.

MEG POKRASS

Some things that reading thousands of very short stories for this anthology have made me believe: Don't be afraid to trust the voice that is distinctly yours. A story, however brief, can contain several turns and still be coherent because, as the poet Richard

Hugo once said, "In the world of imagination, all things belong." Tricks disappoint; the surprise of discovery never does. The wide variety of stories in this anthology is evidence that writing against expectations is nearly always fundamental to success.

GARY FINCKE

PHORADENDRON LEUCARPUM: A MICROFICTION

MICHAEL MARTONE, GUEST EDITOR

"What's that?"

I am directing their attention, the writers in my Introduction to Creative Writing class, to something growing(?), floating(?), caught(?), tangled(?) in the high bare branches of an ancient oak tree.

I like very much "teaching" on a campus in Alabama below the bug line (the line below which insects do not die over winter) because we can walk about and just notice things. I hung that word "teaching" with scare quotes because I don't think what I do is really "teach." I am a big fan of the Russian Formalist, Victor Shklovsky (tonight, at the cocktail party, feel free to drop the name) and his theory of defamiliarization, and, you know, "making the stone stony again."

As we grow up, we lose our sense of wonder as we begin to norm the world, gloss and filter the sensory excesses. We have to do this. We would be overwhelmed by the flood of detailed information if we didn't. Art, making it and consuming it, then, is to notice once more the strangeness of the world we have actively ignored or forgotten we ever knew.

So, back to that walkabout. We walk about the paths and vectors the very same writing students have walked about for the past several years on their way to classes, to work, right by the pink whiskered termite traps, the long abandoned watch key stations, the drab cell antennas drooping from Comer Hall, all having been there already, ready to be seen but edited out of their attending un-attentive attentions.

So what is that, there, up in the old oak tree that, for most of the year, is thick with leaves but now, in the middle of winter, is stripped bare? Bare but for, what (?), these clouds of leaves, still green, that we see now there. They're more than one, and they're like drifts, a matted mash-up of leaves. Or are they nests of some kind, a squirrel's nest someone says, too big for a bird, after saying they have never noticed these things, organically constructed things, before, these thought balloons, thinking of the summer canopy, caught in the upper branches of the old bereft oak.

It's mistletoe.

The white-robed Druids by the bright light of the full moon once harvested mistletoe with golden sickles. Tuscaloosa is also known as Druid City for all its stately oaks most of which are infested with mistletoe. But the name Druid City is suppressed as the Baptist ministers frown on the pagan appellation. Druid City Hospital then is just DCH, and here in town there are no priests with burnished blades. You glean the mistletoe with shotguns.

But wait this little essay is not supposed to be so much about the practice of noticing noticing. Bon voyage, then, Viktor. And not really about mistletoe though as a hemiparasitic plant it has grown on me as a subject, you can see. No, this was to be about a certain species of prose we are calling here Microfiction.

"What's that?"

I am so old, not Druid old but old enough to remember two or three blooms of this prose form. For me it goes back all the way to 1976 and Michel Benedikt's books *Night Cries* and *The Prose Poem: An International Anthology*, the work I recall that produced something that wasn't poetry *per se* or prose *per se* either, that was both lyrical and narrative, real and irreal, and worked, very hard, to frustrate the existential linear nature of written media, creating the illusion, in one page krots of print, that the whole composition, like a painting, was taken in at once by the reader and not one word after another, every golden leaf of the ginkgo dropping at the very same instant.

The serial eruptions of the form that followed, every dozen or so years, always seemed to me to correspond to a cultural generic confidence of the professional critical class that we now know, we're all very certain what's what. What "verse" is and what "fiction" is and what a "story" does and how this "poem" works. These categorizations accelerated as "creative writing" became embedded in the academy with all its classes and classification, its levels and leveling, its gradient grading. We had, we believed figured out what was what with the various and sundry texts, even as the artists that produced "poems" or "stories" there spent more and more of their time in their writing workshops burbling along with critical assessment. But at the moment, at that very moment, when a consensuses had been reached, that moment when we knew that this was that and what was what, Carolyn Forche's ears appear.

I have always been gratified that there isn't that much critical writing written about this kind of writing, that these, what(?), "things" resist being pinned down or even seen. I love that we don't even really know what to call them. Hint. Flash. Micro. Sudden. Blink. Brief. Short Short. They are, whatever they are, by their nature corrosive to criticism, antithetical to thesis. And I must tell you I feel more than a bit conflicted even writing this (what?) this "introduction" that poses, with this gesture of authority, an "introduction" (!), and posits that I have any idea just what is going on here.

Mistletoe. The word origin stems (Ha! *stems*!) from the Old English "dung" and "twig" a shit stick. Yes, the seeds are vectored there by birds as they perch and then work their way beneath the host tree's bark. Mistletoe is hemiparasitic in that its evergreen leaves provide some nutrition through photosynthesis, but its main business is to infiltrate into the vascular system of the host, root into the roots via the branches and the trunk, for nutrition and transpiration.

Perhaps this essay about a fractal form of prose was really about this persistent plant. Or perhaps it's the other way around.

Those Druids were impressed; the compact mat of leaves could bring down an oak. The ancient Ancients as well. Virgil has Aeneas hack from an oak a golden bough that regenerates to carry with him into Hell. I can imagine it this branching tree within the tree's branching branches. Tree-like but not a tree, but, at the same time, more tree than the tree.

How did we ever get it in our heads that a sprig

of the stuff, a start of the start in the oak would magnetize a threshold? A bird sings sweetly in the nether branches of the canopy at the same time delivering from its nether regions an undigested afterthought that, suddenly it seems, grows into a tree in a tree and then into something more than a tree. And somewhere else in some season of death and birth we feel compelled to bend toward each other while calibrating all thirty-four facial muscles and tuning all twelve cranial nerves, both sensory and motor, to kiss, propelled by a cutting or two hung like "scare quotes" on the lintel fashioned from an ancient old oak.

BEST MICROFICTION

HERE ARE THE THINGS THE MOON TOLD ME DURING THE LUNAR ECLIPSE OF JANUARY 21, 2019

ASHELY ADAMS

She appreciates you all standing in the cold to see her. She doesn't mind if you couldn't make it. She doesn't really understand what being cold means, so she'll take your word for it. She's heard a few of you are afraid of staring into the night sky and the forced contemplation of eternity and vastness that comes with it. She thinks, perhaps, you should put yourself in her place, constantly staring at the sweep of earth, that it will help you come to peace with your own smallness. She says to be careful sharing telescopes and binoculars; you'll get pink eye or MRSA. She is, admittedly, unversed in diseases, but knows humanity has a fondness for dripping all over everything. She knows that her light fills you with melancholy and thoughts of those who have passed away. She says to eat that extra slice of pizza. She would be happy to be your big gay wife. She likes all your poems because it's the thought that counts. She wants to know if we still have mammoths or did we get rid of them? She thought mammoths were pretty cool. She wonders why you haven't turned your scars into the shape of rabbits and toads like she's done with her bruises. She assures you the moon landing is not fake. She wants you to know she tries her best to catch all the stones that might kill you. She has never been fond of meteors and their errant catastrophes, a compensation for their eons of lonesome orbits. She would like you to stop saying every lunar eclipse is the end of the world; this is not the end of anything, but a lucky moment where she and the sun and the earth and you fit into each other's shadow.

Ashely Adams is a swamp-adjacent writer whose work has appeared in *Paper Darts*, *Fourth River*, *Permafrost*, *Apex Magazine*, *Cosmonauts Avenue*, and other places. She is the nonfiction editor of the literary journal *Lammergeier*.

HOW TO TELL A STORY FROM THE HEART IN PROPER TIME

RIHAM ADLY

She's in the market in Baghdad bending over a bushel of red onions, a handful of pistachios in one palm and the coins to pay for them in another. When she looks up to pay, she's in a bookstore, a pile of books burdening her arms, books her far-away Americanized brother once read, books that burned her with shame, for not ever, having learned to read. She fumbles for money from her purse but stumbles over the uneven cushions her son messed up. She catches the blare of the T.V. screen, eyes trailing after images of her husband lying dead in a mosque in their new country. Her water breaks and she's giving birth to her son, the son she had to bear, from the man she had to wed. The water in Lake Wanaka has a ghostly sheen. All its fish walled off from her and her son and her brother and … She stares, hands on the T.V. screen, fearful/fearless. She's been trying to get her son to pray regularly in the Mosque or even in Christ's Church. The heart is what matters? No? Where is her son in that flat screen? Or is it her brother? Or is it that fall across the threshold of a half-formed dream back home with her grandma's tales and the painstaking cycles of knitting and embroidery, the careful rolling of vine leaves, the braids long and dark in red ribbons for unwed girls, the Henna nights and ululations for the new bride watching herself pick olives in the blasted fields the American blew up in the war, where the moon runs and the sun chases so fast, so fast, she gasps. She wonders about the heart of things, the heart of words, the heart of Her. One could only meet God Almighty with a pure heart. Did she slow down to love right? To heart? When time is forced to run in the wrong direction, the heart is blinded by the whir of it all, by the spill of semi-formed words blazing like a kite she lost and cannot follow. She sits next to her grandma and nods when she's asked to tell a story—a good story. When she tries to remember, her heart beats so fast, it cries for her to listen and take all the time left and the time given, to weave this tale, right from the heart.

Riham Adly is a fiction writer/translator from Egypt. Her work has appeared in *The Citron Review*, *FlashBack Fiction*, *Vestal Review*, *The Connotation Press*, *Bending Genres*, *New Flash Fiction Review*, *Flash Frontier* and *Ellipsis Zine*, among others. Her stories have received nominations for Best of the Net and the Pushcart Prize.

TED CRUZ ATTENDS A
GOLDFISH FUNERAL

E. KRISTIN ANDERSON

hosted by his youngest daughter, who is seven. He
should have explained to her when she won the fish
at the fair that goldfish sometimes live for a very
long time and sometimes they only live for a little
while. That a goldfish's owner had a responsibility
to care for the goldfish and that this included not
putting dollies in the goldfish bowl—even if the
goldfish seems lonely. Instead Ted has found himself
in a prayer circle around the porcelain toilet while
his little girl tells stories of adventures she had
with this fish that cannot possibly be accurate on
account of it being a fish. Ted considers reminding
her that good little girls don't lie, but suppresses
his instinct just this once. His daughter isn't crying,
though. It's almost as if she doesn't understand
that her pet is, in fact, dead. Facts get blurry when
your brain isn't developed enough to process them.
It's how children see monsters when there's just a
creepy tree making shadows in the window. Real
monsters are human. Ted knows this. He wonders

how many other senators would actually go to a goldfish funeral. He flushes the toilet.

Based in Austin, TX, E. Kristin Anderson is the author of nine chapbooks, including *A Guide for the Practical Abductee*, *Pray, Pray, Pray: Poems I wrote to Prince in the middle of the night*, *17 seventeen XVII* and *Behind, All You've Got*. Kristin is a poetry reader at *Cotton Xenomorph* and an editorial assistant at *Sugared Water*.

ONE DAY AN ORGASM DECIDES TO MOVE TO SPAIN

NIN ANDREWS

to leave this country behind and reinvent herself in another landscape and language, but she can't figure out how to be an orgasm in Spanish. Her travel guide speaks only of *el orgasmo*. Do the Spanish not know *la orgasma*? And why not? After all, cats are both *el gato* and *la gata*, and they even have little *gatitos*, so shouldn't orgasms come in both genders? And have little *orgasmitos*?

Reading a little further, she wonders if an orgasm is simply *there* in Spain, as in: *Hay la orgasma.* No verb necessary. She likes that idea. The simplicity that she, the orgasm, could merely exist. She pictures a curtain opening to applause as she steps into the spotlight and takes a bow, her red hair sweeping the floor.

But then she wonders, how did she get there? Was she *had* by another, as in English? *Tuvo una orgasma?* She's so tired of being had. Why can't she simply be? But what form of *to be* would she be? *Ser* or *estar?*

She thinks, *ser*. She tries it out as soon as she arrives in the airport in Madrid. *Hola*, she announces, *Yo soy la orgasma*. The people turn away. Some even break into a run, their suitcase wheels squealing behind them.

How lonely she feels then. Eavesdropping on passersby, she hears one say, *Estoy muerto*. In speaking of death, she realizes, one uses the verb, *estar*. Death, it turns out, is an ongoing condition in Spain. If death is ongoing, then surely the orgasm is too—both of them being the all-too familiar, uninvited guests in the backs of people's minds. Just thinking of this, the orgasm grows sad. *Estoy triste*, she sighs. How lovely that sounds. *Triste*. Like a tree of stars.

Nin Andrews' poems have appeared in many literary journals and anthologies including *Ploughshares*, *Agni*, *The Paris Review*, and four editions of *Best American Poetry*. She is the author of seven chapbooks and seven full-length poetry collections. Her next book, *The Last Orgasm*, is forthcoming from Etruscan Press.

FROM THE SLUMBARAVE HOTEL ON BROADWAY

JULES ARCHER

The hotel key was ours. A rectangular piece of hard plastic with the words PLAY SLEEP REPEAT on the front. New York City. That humid summer day when it rained frogs and people shielded themselves with their umbrellas, only to be pelted anyway. Four concussions. One death. And us? We were snug in our suite. Plush pillows, silk sheets, turndown service. A mini bar we emptied. We filled that hotel room with the scent of weed, of sex. When we parted ways, I slipped the key into my purse. I'd never let the front desk shred it, erase its memory, cavalierly toss it away, whatever one does with a used hotel key. That night when I went home, I placed the key on my nightstand. Sat it upright, braced by a bottle of La Mer hand cream. When my husband came to bed, I reached for him and gave him a kiss. He didn't notice the key. He would never notice the key. Instead, he pet me like a child and said goodnight.

Jules Archer is the author of the chapbook, *All the Ghosts We've*

Always Had (Thirty West Publishing, 2018) and the short story collection, *Little Feasts* (Thirty West Publishing, 2020). Her writing has appeared in various journals, including *SmokeLong Quarterly*, *Pank*, *Maudlin House*, and elsewhere.

THE THING

COLETTE ARRAND

I came to occupy this skin by accident. To which drugs do I attribute my healthy glow? Once, I was asked if I missed my religion & I said I took the Eucharist every day: eight milligrams of estradiol under the tongue, 100 milligrams of spironolactone down my throat, & the knowledge that bodies are not immutable objects. Before this, my skin ruptured & oozed; my face reddened like an alcoholic's because I am an alcoholic. None of my flaws are obvious. (That's why it's called concealer.) The pictures on my dating profile are old so thank god you just want to know how hung I am. Invent my dimensions; I'll try to make them work. You'll never know. When I say *six inches* I mean *a gentleman's three*. When I say *size 16* I'm being generous. When I say *come closer* I'm saying that I want to disappear you into one of my many mouths. At night, I'm as good as the real thing. In the morning, I can be whoever you need me to be.

Colette Arrand is the author of *The Future Is Here and Every-*

thing Must Be Destroyed (Split Lip Press, 2019) and *Hold Me Gorilla Monsoon* (OPO Books and Objects, 2017). She lives in Athens, Georgia.

THE GRAND AM

TYLER BARTON

His mother said a good cry grew in your gut—a bad cry, in your brain. She'd always fail to calm him by insisting there was a difference. *Don't worry, Lovey, this is a good one.* Good cries held a glass of wine, a book face down across the thigh. A good cry wore proper shoes: fuzzy socks with rubber floor grips. A good cry involved the dog, regal, sitting tall beside her, an ivory thing she reached for, to steady herself, a cane.

Bad cries were things she hid. They happened in the Pontiac. Driver's seat. 9:45 pm. Just home from work. Headlights off. Seatbelt still buckled. He'd watch her from the window beside his pillow. Down there. Where the only light was the winking red eye of the Marlboro. How it shook in her hand. Grand-Am filling with smoke. When she finally crept inside, he was as bad at feigning sleep as she was at pretending to believe him.

Tonight—his stomach growling, blood pulsing in both temples—he wants to call her. Not to apologize, not to answer the question of why he never calls, but to ask for a diagnosis. *Mom, listen*. Tell me which this is.

Tyler Barton is a co-founder of Fear No Lit, home of the Submerging Writer Fellowship. His collection of flash fiction, *The Quiet Part Loud*, won the Turnbuckle Chapbook prize from Split Lip Press. Find his short stories in *The Iowa Review*, *Kenyon Review*, *Gulf Coast*, and more. Find him at @goftyler or tsbarton.com

THE HORSES ARE READY AND THEY NEED TO GO

CHRISTOPHER CITRO

What I ate with my coffee. How I felt about the slack rope. What I remembered from the rivers of my youth, the mud and catfish. It's a gearing up just to speak as the self. How do I feel about the pines in the front yard? Yes, Mahler, but what about after the Mahler? I love to hear you clinking things in another room.

In the year we've been here, you've rearranged your studio maybe four times. Me, so far, none. I know I need help. I'm just not programmed to know how to give it to myself. Now all I have to do is remember that when I need it.

Twenty minutes ago I held your body between my lips.

I can put my hand to my mouth.

Someone's painting horses pouring across a valley floor. It's been done before. They don't care. They're doing it again.

Christopher Citro is the author of *If We Had a Lemon We'd Throw It and Call That the Sun* (Elixir Press, 2020), winner of the 2019 Antivenom Award, and *The Maintenance of the Shimmy-Shammy* (Steel Toe Books, 2015). He teaches creative writing at SUNY Oswego and lives in Syracuse, NY.

WEIGHT ROOM

PAUL CRENSHAW

I never liked the clink of heavy weights or the expelling of heavy breaths, the way we boys maneuvered as men around the weight room, lifting things and setting them down again just to show we could. I didn't like the big belts that were supposed to protect our small backs from all the heavy lifting, nor the jocks we strapped on to protect our most private parts. I didn't like the adrenaline and anger some boys aimed at the weights, as if gravity were designed to keep them down. I didn't like how fights broke out afterward, how we grunted like apes, how, in the bathroom, there was always a turd someone thought would be funny not to flush.

But what I hated most was the way, after a while, our bodies began changing. The big among us got bigger, and stronger, able to lift more and more, until they thought, there in their small skins, that all it took to lift the world was strength.

Paul Crenshaw is the author of the essay collections *This One Will Hurt You*, published by The Ohio State University Press, and *This We'll Defend*, from the University of North Carolina Press. Other work has appeared in *Best American Essays*, *Best American Nonrequired Reading*, *The Pushcart Prize*, *Oxford American*, *Glimmer Train*, and *Tin House*.

HERE

TOMMY DEAN

We all live poorly here. Use mail-in rebates at the hardwood store, get drunk at Sammy's on Friday nights, and let our children run around in their underwear in our front yards. They wave flags, swords, and guns, practicing for the coming days when soldier is the only job that comes with benefits.

We all live insecurely here. Guns unlocked and loaded, resting oily beneath dusty bed-ruffles, front doors with deadbolts and chains, evidence of forced entry too cracked to paint over, pharmacy and liquor store heavily gated and watched by paid-by-the-hour security guards turtled with bullet-proof vests.

We all live indignantly here. Dig up stop signs and hammer them into the walls above our beds, siphon cable from the trailer court terminal, dig up surveyor stakes, forcing our pets to defecate on imaginary property lines, hoist cars up on jacks in our front drives, license plates conspicuously missing.

We all live rashly here. Spending the last of our paychecks at VFW fish fry's, McDonalds' Happy Meals, and on the spirits of amnesia: vodka, marijuana, and oxy. We roll through town timing belts squealing, humming along to 107.3 Classic rock, looking anywhere but the fuel gauge, hollering through the stripped-soul ache of being unknown. We race trains and semis, dart through intersections, collecting unacknowledged badges of goddamn luck, leaving rashes of side panel paint everywhere we go.

We all live permanently here. Football Friday nights, performing art center dance recitals, candle-light vigils for missing tweens, bake sale Saturdays for mission trips and recess equipment, petitions for crosswalks and longer traffic lights. Car crashes, lightning strikes, and messy affairs whisper through the corn-arrowed fields.

We all live ignorantly here. Making references to our ancestors, those that scattered the ashes of cultures they couldn't bring to a caged harmony. Claiming a land that was never promised, that continues to seep with miasmas of chemical cocktails, evolution feasting on its own tail. We stockpile weapons, hell-bent on protecting our ideals of liberty while riding the twin thoroughbreds of abhorrence and distrust, proclaiming an erosive happiness. This, we say, is the only way to live.

Tommy Dean lives in Indiana with his wife and two children. He is the Flash Fiction Editor at *Craft*. His story "You've Stopped" was chosen by Dan Chaon to be included in *Best Microfiction 2019* and was also included in *Best Small Fictions 2019*. Find him @TommyDeanWriter on Twitter.

MEN'S SECRETS

LEONORA DESAR

It happened when I was 15. All of a sudden I was hot. It came out of nowhere. One minute I was invisible and the next boys were feeling me up behind the stairs. They always say, don't let strangers touch you, but they weren't strangers. They were sopho-mores. Their names were Alan, Billy, Steve. They wore braces. Mullets. They said, *let's get this party started*. After a while they said nothing. They just did a little thing, like their legs were walking, which was code, for stairwell. We went. Usually there was a lot of tongue involved. Then the hands would start. They went up the shirt. Down the shirt. They paused at the pants and then they went there, too. They hung out. They said, *hello*, like *we are giving you the pleasure of your life*. It always stopped there, strangely. It's like they read a book up to a certain point, and then Mom came in. After that things were formal. We sat there like nuns, or teachers. It was all very chivalrous, really. He would hold the door for me and we would go into whatever happened next, chemistry class, maybe, or the yard. Then he would ignore me and I would ignore him, or pretend to, I did what my dad does, I'd say, *time does not exist except for at this moment*. I looked around and murdered time. Then I took the bus.

By 11th grade we just looked at each other. It was like a formality, like a favorite TV show you can't give up, even though it's in the 7th season and all the main characters have died. It was as if he'd forgotten how to feel. He was lost. He was thinking about algebra or how our teacher looked like Humpty Dumpty. It interfered with things, like sex. He put his hand over my blouse and we just sat there. And in the end he gave me this look, like *don't tell Steve or Billy*. I nodded. It would be our secret. It was a bond. I told myself this. It smelled like M&M's and menthols, like $x=y2$. He was the x and I the y, or he the y, it didn't matter—we equaled out. My mother looked at me. She said, *there's something different about you*, and I nodded. I was a woman now. I knew how to keep men's secrets.

Leonora Desar's writing has appeared in *River Styx*, *Passages North*, *Black Warrior Review*, *Mid-American Review*, *Best Microfiction 2019*, *The Best Small Fictions 2019*, *Wigleaf* and Wigleaf's Top 50, among others. She won third place in *River Styx*'s 2018 microfiction contest, and was a finalist/runner-up in *Crazyhorse*'s Crazyshorts! contest.

SWANS MAY BITE WITHOUT WARNING

MELANIE DIXON

I'm running and I'm running and I'm running, and my legs are pounding and my heart is thumping and I'm running along the Heathcote River and my feet are hitting the ground and my heart is thudding and I'm running and I'm running and I'm running through the Ernle Clark reserve, and there's a black and white dog running in front of me, and it's not my dog and it's running and I'm running and it's running, and the branches above me are being pushed around by the winter breeze, and the Heathcote is bubbling towards Beckenham then St Martins and I'm running and I'm running and I'm running, and a fantail loops in front of me and it's flying and I'm running and it's flying and the cold air stings my eyes and my eyes are watering and I'm not crying, I'm not crying, I'm not crying, and my feet are thumping the ground, and I run into a puddle and the mud splashes the back of my legs and I'm running and I'm running and I'm running and the sign says, *Swans may bite without warning*, and a family of shelducks with six ducklings paddle in the field behind the fence and they're paddling and I'm running and I'm running and I'm running and I don't see any swans and nothing bites me and nothing hurts me and I'm not crying, it's just me and my legs and my feet and my heart, and I'm running and I'm running and I'm running.

Melanie Dixon is a short story writer, novelist and poet, with work published and anthologised internationally. Based in Christchurch, New Zealand, she is a graduate of Hagley Writers' Institute, and is a student on the Masters of Creative Writing programme at the University of Auckland.

HER WING

CATHERINE EDMUNDS

One of her wings falls off, and she's like, "Whatever." I tell her I've been to the shop and didn't get even mildly stabbed. She's not interested. I show her my cow shoes, like those worn by moonshiners in the Prohibition days to disguise their footprints. She's chewing gum, and sometimes there's a slight slapping sound from her mouth. I don't know how to help her. This is the thing with agony; it can present as boredom.

I burn the sausages, the way she likes them, but when I go to tell her tea's ready, she's gone. Her wing is lying on the sofa, dusty and slightly greasy, smelling of lanolin. I don't know what to do with it.

I live through the seasons, I grow old. I fold the wing carefully and put it in the attic. One day she might need it again. She could fly to heaven with that wing. I have to believe.

Catherine Edmunds is a writer, artist and folk/rock fiddle player. Her published works include two poetry collections, four novels and a Holocaust memoir. She has been nominated three times for a Pushcart Prize, shortlisted in the Bridport four times, and has works in journals including *Aesthetica*, *Crannóg* and *Ambit*.

STILL WARM

K. M. ELKES

The boy sits at the top of the stairs and waits for the smell to come. He is familiar with the kitchen scene below—a fat turd of ground meat smokes in a pan, his mother leans on the counter, the edge whitening ridges into her palms. The high shriek of the extractor fan, extracting.

Across the landing, his father grimaces round a shaving brush, then dips his razor and draws it down his neck. The boy remembers the stubble noise on his father's collar when he used to kiss him good-night. Alive and mysterious, like radio static. His father looks at the boy, then double taps his razor on the sink and toes the bathroom door shut.

The boy slides down three more stairs, settles and waits.

Recipe For A Boy's Lunch:

One slice of thin white bread, unbuttered.
Ground pork or sausage-meat, fried the colour of night.
A shake or two of ketchup.
One slice of thin white bread, unbuttered.

His father says that she cries and stares and lies in darkened bedrooms with a damp flannel over her brow because she is a woman of a certain age, weak with her nerves. That whatever they do, they are quiet. That they do not disturb. His father says none of this is the boy's fault. Except, the way he says it, it is.

The boy slides down three more, settles, waits. He idles against the pale ribs of the bannister until he is finally called into the kitchen. Smoke hangs low as early morning mist. He remembers, as he always does, to say thank you as the wrapped sandwich is handed to him. It has the weight of a human heart.

His mother wets her fingers and slicks down a rogue lock on the boy's head, then sighs and kisses a cheek and tells him to behave himself. She smells of burnt meat.

Five years hungry, that boy. Yet as he sets off for school, he takes the same care as always, the same love as always, when he feeds a neighbour's bin with that wrapped and blackened heart, inedible and still warm.

K. M. Elkes is the author of the flash collection *All That Is Between Us* (Ad Hoc Fiction, 2019). His flash stories have won or been placed in many competitions, including Bath Flash Award, Reflex Fiction Prize, Fish Publishing Prize and the Bridport Prize. He's been published in over 50 anthologies and literary magazines.

STAINED LIPS

JAN ELMAN STOUT

She dabs her lips with *Faithful Fawn*. He hovers behind, runs his fingers through his graying hair, eyes fixed on his reflection. *How do I look?* Her mouth forms a perfect "O," presses shut. *Handsome.* He points. *When you move your mouth that way, you look like a fish.* Her mind recedes to their rehearsal dinner. The baby photos her mother had blown up. *Adorable*, she'd said when she saw his. *Your forehead's so high*, he'd responded. She drops her stained tissue in the toilet. Flushes. *What's that lip color?* he asks. *Fawn*, she answers, and flashes her broad smile.

Jan Elman Stout's fiction has appeared in *Pure Slush*, *Literary Orphans*, *Jellyfish Review*, *Midwestern Gothic*, *Midway Journal*, *Lost Balloon*, *100 Word Story*, and elsewhere. Her flash has been nominated for the Best Small Fictions anthology in 2017, 2018, 2019 and 2020. Jan is a Senior Editor at *SmokeLong Quarterly*.

A QUICK WORD ABOUT MY LIFE

TRENT ENGLAND

Ever since they opened up a falling club in our town, there's little else that Theresa will do. After her daily shift at the ball bearing plant, she drives to the large, lime-stained building that used to be a Toys "R" Us, where she falls into foam pits, backwards, as though she's a concertgoer in a mosh pit or a toppled statue of a despot. Like a gym, it has its members and regulars and Theresa remembers everyone's names. Over dinner, she tells me about Dan who falls because he has a stressful job as a 911 operator or Janet who has three children to feed and thinks that any day her husband will get fired. I hear about Becki who sleeps with night terrors and Greg who can't sleep at all. And while she's telling me that if she falls enough she will one day earn a spot in the platinum level, which is the old stock room, and get to step off backwards from an even greater height, I wonder what she tells Dan and Janet and Becki and Greg about her own life or about me, or why, for example, when she leaves work to drive to the falling club, she passes our house without stopping, without looking up at the window to see her husband standing there.

Trent England's work has appeared in a number of literary journals including *Conjunctions*, *Bull*, and *Hobart*. When he is not writing, he is working as a stay-at-home dad. He lives in Boston with his wife Denise and his son Wilder, and can be found online at tengland.com.

THE BOOK OF X: VISION #13 (THROAT FIELDS)

SARAH ROSE ETTER

I took my lover out to the throat fields because I need something to strangle.

"It'll be five dollars per throat," a man in overalls calls to us and I pay.

"It's been a long week at work," I explain.

"I don't understand," he says.

Discomfort blares off his skin in the sun. This is his first time, and I want it to be tender.

The bare necks reach toward the sun, short stalks of flesh, the raw edges of the throats blooming the color of old blood at the center.

How did he see me before this? Poised with the right hair. Now, I am disheveled, wearing filthy sweats, bags under eyes.

Lately, the fury has been keeping me up. My anger boils under my skin at work, beneath the fluorescent lights of the office. All I have ever wanted is a soft place. At night, I dream of rooms filled with feathers or cotton.

"You don't feel the same anymore, do you?" I ask

him out in the throat fields.

I can feel his ebbs and flows instantly. I know when he is turning from me in the slightest way, as if a flower toward another sun.

"Remember the good days?" I ask.

He looks carved as stone. No words, just that straight face.

"Say something," I say.

The silence is bigger than suns, it is the silence of distant galaxies. The universe begins to crumble. The rage roars trucklike through my blood.

I throw myself to my knees in the field. I grab a good neck, a thick neck. I look up at him with my mania. The rage multiplies and I wrap fingers around the flesh.

"SAY SOMETHING," I scream.

I clench hard, good around the throat. I squeeze until my fingers want to break. The skin caves in beneath, which feels good, a satisfaction. I strangle harder, until I go dizzy from lack of oxygen, until my rage deflates.

I pant on the ground before him, my weak fingers still around the skin. He stands in the field, still silent, immobile. I stare up at his throat which is long and thick, glinting in the light like a silver coin.

Sarah Rose Etter is the author of *Tongue Party*, selected by Deb Olin Unferth as the winner of the Caketrain Press award, and *The Book of X*, her first novel. Her work has appeared or is forthcoming in *The Cut*, *Electric Literature*, *Guernica*, *VICE*, *New York Tyrant*, *Juked*, *Night Block*, *The Black Warrior Review*, *Salt Hill Journal*, *The Collagist*, and elsewhere.

WHY I LOVE PENGUINS

MFC FEELEY

Back when I had to reach high for her hand, everyone thought my mother was a cop. I don't know if it was her clinical gaze or that she found the false friendliness of California obscene, but she retained an authority from her days as head nurse that made people tremble like they'd left socks on the kitchen floor. Everywhere we went, secretaries terminated personal calls, herbalists hid their pot, and jay-walkers corrected course. One jaywalker, freezing in the street, got hit by a VW Bug. My mother administered triage until the ambulance came.

Against the hippies, my mother gleamed like an icicle, sharpening in the swelter of '69. Men chased her shade, and she wanted a man, but fear of arrest halted their advance. This constant harassment, coupled with frustration, increased my mother's taste for being alone. Silent in ribbons and Mary-Janes, I traveled, safe as a wallet, inside her psychic shield.

But her favored escape—cigarettes—made men comfortable. Between men offering her lights and men trying to distract her from their partner's petty crimes, she could never puff in peace. Until one day, at the zoo, when one too many men asked if she wasn't really a stalking panther, she spied a shady nook in the penguin house.

Straightening her back, she clasped my hand and turned the latch on the almost invisible door carved through the wall of artificial ice. The penguins raised a fuss, but no one questioned us. We waded through flapping fish and sat on a slimy rock.

Still wearing her gloves, my mother took out her crushed pack of Winstons while I patted the friendlier penguins, all of whom I named Sid, on the head. I expected squelchy patent-leather, but found their craniums soft to the touch. My mother smoked in glorious peace. I flapped my wings and fell in the water.

Walking home, the smell of guano, our dripping dresses, and my bloody shins (where—understandably—Sid bit me for plucking his feathers), kept the men at bay. My mother stripped off her ruined kidskin and pointed at trees and flowers; ribbons of smoke trailed from her cigarette and, when I stopped to pet a caterpillar with my penguin feather, she squeezed my hand.

MFC Feeley wrote a series of ten stories inspired by the Bill of Rights for *Ghost Parachute* and has published in *SmokeLong*, *Jellyfish Review*, *Brevity Blog*, *Liar's League*, and others. More at MFC Feeley/Facebook and on Twitter MFC Feeley @FeeleyMfc

SHE WILL BECOME A BIRD SCIENTIST

JENNY FERGUSON

Rose will blame her stepfather for the path she's on, a dry smile animating her lips. He will be an old man by then, but he will still talk about the time they drove to Coaldale and walked through the Centre, and Snoopy the Turkey Vulture captured her interest more than the eagles, owls, or hawks. The vulture with its pink-red face, stained by nature to blend its feathers with the insides of its meals. It flies in circles, wobbling in the air as it inhales death. In preparation to study it, she will learn Spanish. She will live in South America, in its ancestral home, during the winters, returning to Alberta only during the summer when the bird breeds. Her stepfather fed it, this possibility, on a Saturday when Rose was twelve, maybe thirteen. Her boyfriends will brag to their friends about the places where she lays her head in winters, about the surf on the coasts, and inland, the forests, jungles, the trees like nothing Canada has to offer. None of them will last a research season.

Jenny Ferguson is Métis, an activist, a feminist, an auntie, and an accomplice with a PhD. She believes writing and teaching are political acts. *Border Markers*, her collection of linked flash fiction narratives, is available from NeWest Press.

HOW MY PARENTS, WHO GAVE ME UP FOR ADOPTION, MIGHT HAVE MET

EPIPHANY FERRELL

1. She was a dog groomer and he had an Airedale terrier that bit everyone who attempted to pluck his coat as the dog breed standards suggest. She was able to turn shag to glamour. Her secret, she said, was feeding the dog a tuna melt before and during grooming. He loved her ingenuity. They shared a kiss over the stainless steel grooming table, they shared more than a kiss. Then he left for the supposed easy money of oil rig work in the Gulf, and she prepared for law school, a destination she absolutely had to enter child-free.

2. He sat in her section at Smiley Guys and she served him a few extra boneless wings whenever he'd come in because she knew money was a problem for him while he waited to pitch his invention to the GM executives. But it was when he got a taste of her made-from-scratch key lime pie that he declared his love for her and they

planned to run away together. The unexpected and months-too-soon pregnancy brought clarity. He left town to pitch for a minor-minor league farm team, and she moved to a part of the world where she would hear no echo of him.

3. They were married, each to someone else. They made a single exception to fidelity.

4. They were married, each to someone else. They felt safe-ish together. And in one night of excesses—too much alcohol, too much moonlight, too much opportunity—they covered each other's fears. The morning sun squeezed the moonlight out of the room, and came between them like daggers.

5. They were going to marry, years ago. He changed his mind. She didn't want the souvenir.

6. They were married, each to someone else. No one had ever called her "honey." No one had ever called him "darlin'."

7. They didn't ask each other the right questions.

8. They were married, each to someone else. Her husband was nearing the end of his battle with a long illness. She was soul-weary, sick of heart. He'd always thought there was more to her than she let on. He was right. It was a whirlwind. After the funeral, she fled upstate and never

returned. He never stopped thinking about her. He did not attend her funeral, a decade later. He didn't even know she had died.

Epiphany Ferrell received a Pushcart nomination in 2018, and her stories have appeared recently in *The Slag Review*, *New Flash Fiction Review*, *Pulp Literature*, and other places. She blogs intermittently at *Ghost Parachute* and is on the editorial staff at *Mojave River Review*. She lives and writes near the Shawnee Forest.

TEETH

TIM FITTS

Fishing in the Gulf, and the sonar isn't working. We see the digital interference on the screen, but it turns out to be rocks, or seaweed, or fish—fish that don't bite or won't bite or don't feel like biting, but fish. Somebody tells me I should not have brought along bananas. How am I to know which random food to bring or not bring? But as it happens at sea, your luck changes. To our right, a sea bird dives in, no splash, no sound. Our first catch is grouper. One after the other. Keep the big ones, toss the babies. I hook a black bass by the tongue, another through the gills. We haul in a succession of grunts, reds, and sheepshead. The sheepshead teeth so wide and dull they don't look like a sheep's head at all, they look like a fish's head, but grafted with the mouth of an old man, like an old man who's been drinking coffee and smoking his entire life and bragging to his friends that he doesn't do a damn thing for his teeth. Doesn't brush, doesn't floss. Doesn't go to the dentist, but look, they're all here.

Tim Fitts lives in Philadelphia where he teaches in the Liberal Arts Department of the Curtis Institute of Music. He is the author of two short story collections, and his stories have been published by journals such as *Granta*, *The Gettysburg Review*, *Apple Valley Review*, *Boulevard*, *New South*, among many others.

WE DIVE

SARAH FRELIGH

Age 12, we dive and dive. For the girl playing dead by the drain in the deep end of the pool. For the pennies we toss in the water by the lifeguard's chair. From the diving board: three steps, the hurdle, the launch. We come up for air long enough to eat lunch, cheeseburgers and fries drowned in a murder of ketchup. Our bellies, humped and rounded, push against the elastic of our bathing suits as we dive and dive and dive.

At 14, we lie in the gutters of the swimming pool, basting our bellies in baby oil and the occasional wavelets of cool that slop up whenever someone dives in. We pick at burgers without buns, drink cans of Tab poured warm over ice that cracks like knuckles. We learn about calories and fat from the high school girls who shout warnings across the humid locker room. Sometimes we dive but only at the end of the day.

At 18, we arrange chaise lounges and serve up the buffet of ourselves, tasty swell of breasts basted to brown, a feast for the boys teeing off on the first hole. Later we pull out hand mirrors and paint alien faces over our own eyes and lips, wait by the 18th green while they putt out. We prop our feet on the dashboard of their cars, let them drive us to a rutted field off a dirt road where we unzip and dive as if we are starving. We hold our breath, but we've already smothered. Already drowned.

Sarah Freligh is the author of *Sad Math*, winner of the 2014 Moon City Press Poetry Prize and the 2015 Whirling Prize from the University of Indianapolis. She is the recipient of poetry fellowships from the National Endowment for the Arts and the Constance Saltonstall Foundation.

SICK DAY

SCOTT GARSON

He takes a sick day. He isn't feeling well, he explains to his wife in a text. You're sick? she responds. He looks at the words on his phone. He keys an emoji, a shrug. I feel untogether, he writes.

Untogether with me?

No! he replies, adding hearts.

The truth is a feeling. He'd been reassigned to a distant building—Pre-Owned Vehicles. His cubicle entry faces a plug-in fountain whose pump is not set right; rather than ambient trickle, it yields an erratic drip. He works through call backs—low odds stuff, he fears—with increasingly alien zeal. The supervisor, Vickie Beer, has a go-to saying: it ebbs and flows. Meaning business. Life. Anything. He likes her easy, booming laugh and the way she leans to listen and nod when he is responding to her. Still, he's concerned. For the past few days, he has sensed some difference. Like he's not there. Or she doesn't see him. Or sees him just as a thought, just in the moment of passing.

He sweeps the patio.

The day is an emptiness.

He walks, takes a path through the woods. When his daughter is born and starts to grow, he'll take her on walks of this kind, he thinks. He'll teach her to locate sassafras; they'll bend to rinse leaves in the brook.

But now that he's made the turn in his mind toward the future, he feels—again? disintegration. Mute, like dread.

Like actual nausea.

He's tried to tell himself that he's just paranoid, that he's imagining things. But he's not. He knows this—all at once. He knows what he saw in Vickie Beer's eye as she passed without looking his way: a glitch, a disturbance—tied, he understands, to knowledge not yet shared.

She'll call him into her office tomorrow. Just as she would have today. She'll ask him to sit. He can see the firm chair in his mind. He will have time to station his hands. He will have time to settle his breath, to conform. It won't be personal.

Scott Garson is the author of *Is That You, John Wayne?*—a collection of stories. He lives in central Missouri.

LAFAYETTE, INDIANA

SARAH GREEN

In Lafayette, Indiana, in 2003, sometimes the
air smelled like steamed milk for no reason. The
restaurant with the best enchiladas was tacked to
a used-car sales lot. I swear a bead curtain marked
the line between them. But maybe nothing marked
it. In winter, on the same block as a tattoo parlor
named Redemption, neighbors left unlit reindeer
out for weeks, grazing. They must have looked
like constellations at night, but it was always day
when I saw them, their bodies just wire with space
between. You had to imagine the light. You had
to imagine they could smell something under the
snow, something earthen; thawing grass blades. In
Lafayette, Indiana by the stockyards sometimes the
air smelled like Purina. Sometimes the air smelled
like soy beans. The wind would change and it would
feel dangerous again to walk anywhere with him
trying to pass for the first time as a boy. His Chaplin
saunter and track jacket, long eyelashes. Always a
pack of men leaning outside of the video store, the
gas station. His "do you think they think...?" One
time I grabbed the fabric of his white t-shirt, playing,

and he was furious, as if I'd torn part of a photo-
graph in which the shirt held him: vintage, correct.
We tore apart. In Lafayette, Indiana, sometimes the
air smelled like burnt sugar at 3 AM, despite no
lights on at the bakery. Somewhere, the reindeer's
ribs and shoulders glimmering.

Sarah Green is the author of *Earth Science: poems* (421 Atlanta)
and the editor of *Welcome to the Neighborhood: An Anthology
of American Coexistence* (Ohio University Press). Her work has
appeared in *Best New Poets*, the Pushcart Prize anthology,
32 Poems, *Paris Review*, *FIELD*, *Copper Nickel*, *Pleiades*, and
elsewhere.

AN IMAGINARY NUMBER
for Gwendolyn

SIÂN GRIFFITHS

That night, she danced with aliens. They spoke to her in math. In school, she was learning multiplication tables and isolation; she understood whispers as sound waves measuring the distance between planets. School math was rote. Alien math worked on another logic, requiring no memory. Their three-step time altered her heart's beat.

Though the waltz was a one-time thing, it was an instant that stretched its roots through her past and budded tendrils into every moment of her future. Just as in English *cleave* can mean parting or coming together, their language allowed one time, simultaneously, to be all time. Or perhaps it was simply the nature of moments to be both fleeting and forever. There was no telling.

The dance tempo was determined by her body, which unlike theirs was bound to the earth and the moon and the rotations of the sun, a concept of time born in a body brought up by those celestial bodies. Each step marked a moment between birth and death, between here and there, between alien and familiar. She knew love from her parents, though work took them daily. These new beings took her hands in their appendages. They matched their rhythms to hers, and then allowed rhythm to evolve, solving an equation. Rooms away, her parents stirred, though the music in the room was soundless.

What called them to her from across the stars? She did not know. When the aliens returned from whence they came, she was no longer one lonely girl but, rather, a girl for whom loneliness had become an imaginary number, a girl whose understanding stretched to contain galaxies, a girl whose limbs, even now, contain that once-waltz.

Siân Griffiths teaches creative writing at Weber State University. Her work has appeared in *The Georgia Review*, *Prairie Schooner*, *Booth*, *American Short Fiction*, and other publications. Her second novel *Scrapple* and her short fiction chapbook *The Heart Keeps Faulty Time* are forthcoming in 2020. For more information, please visit sbgriffiths.com

The Journal of
Compressed Creative Arts

ESCAPE INTO THE
WAKING WORLD

MARY GRIMM

Kathy puts her cup down, one more cup of the
thousands we have drunk together, this cup, white
with a blue band, down on the table between us. I
used to think I had it in me to do something, she
says. I used to think there was something ahead that
would take everything I had. Now one day to the
next is all I can handle. Everybody's lunch. Everybody's socks. Fucking shopping four times a week.

Outside there is a little boy starting a fire on a
driveway, not either of ours, thank god, not the
driveway, not the boy. He has a magnifying glass,
the kind that is meant to be held over a book, square,
with a handle.

I hate to go home, Kathy says, there's no control.
I murmur yes, yes, and we agree that home is
chaos, home is a whirlpool that is always sucking
you down, floating with egg-crusted plates, grass-
stained pants, toasters that will toast only on one
side so that you must turn the bread and turn it
until it is the right shade of brown, the right shade

that can be eaten without someone claiming it will make him throw up.

Yes, Kathy says, I hate to go home. I think that I think that she doesn't really mean it.

At work Kathy wears a bathing suit, swims through the air at the side of the pool, encouraging the water-bound exercisers. She smiles, gleaming blonde in her blue suit, calling on the twenty-plus women to breathe deep, to love their own movement through the water. Now though, trapped in the sulky air of the kitchen, we cling to the handles of our cups. Something is chasing us, something dreamed and fanciful, but maybe also real.

I know it doesn't matter, Kathy says. Everything is the same in the end. Her cigarette smoke drifts, smelling like heated caramel and burnt rubber.

I have nothing to say, nothing I want to say. I am thinking about sweat flesh sex, about trying as we do for the perfect new body, too late now for metaphysical fitness, too late for beauty, but still.

Mary Grimm has had two books published, *Left to Themselves* (novel) and *Stealing Time* (story collection)—both by Random House. Currently, she is working on a dystopian novel about oldsters. She teaches fiction writing at Case Western Reserve University.

AN INVENTORY OF THE POSSESSIONS OF WILLIAM KEVIN THOMPSON, JR., AGE 19, UPON HIS EXPULSION FROM THE FAMILY RESIDENCE ON OCTOBER 20, 1971

THADDEUS GUNN

Mad magazine no. 125, March 1969

Playboy magazine, December 1968

Big Daddy Ed Roth "Rat Fink" "Drag Nut" high-impact plastic model by Revell, completed

Syringes, hypodermic

Dried rose arrangement

Laura Morell's high school graduation picture, torn

Tales of the Cthulhu Mythos by HP Lovecraft, Ballantine Books

A dog-eared copy of the *Bhagavad Gita*, publisher unknown

Cannabis sativa, two grams

Enfield .303 SMLE Mark III rifle plus 20 rounds soft-point ammunition

Fetal pig, preserved in formaldehyde

US Army surplus down-filled mummy bag, olive drab

Glue, Testors brand model cement

India ink, two ounces

Jelly jars of bolts, washers, and ball bearings

Xerox copy of xanthomonas colloidal mixture techniques for homemade napalm, gelignite, and plastique from *The Anarchist Cookbook* by William Powell

KA-BAR US Marine Corps issue tactical knife

Yellow legal pads, three

Winchester 12-gauge shotgun

Handwritten on scrap paper: haiku, free verse, and diagrams of the back door, driveway, and basement entry of the family residence

Sawed-off .22 rifle of indeterminate manufacture

Notice of determination regarding the application for conscientious objector status

Order receipt from Ward Scientific for two pounds of ammonium perchlorate

Zen symbols enso and yin yang, hand brushed on papyrus

"Quantiferous amounts" (his words) of anhydrous ether in a brown glass bottle

Valentine's Day greeting card, dated February 14, 1962, handmade, crayon and construction paper with message "I am sory for all the rong I have done" signed Billy

---

Thaddeus Gunn's work has appeared in *The Kenyon Review*, *Tin House*, *Brevity*, *SmokeLong Quarterly*, and elsewhere. He is currently working on a memoir.

ALICE IN NEVERLAND

KYLE HEMMINGS

In a room two doors over from the boyfriend's mother, Alice peels this morning's skirt and paisley blouse. As if losing herself in a silent prayer of her own making, she's going to give up the remaining fragments of her virginity. Simple as shedding a paper dress, a ditsy friend drunk on plum wine once told her.

Alice wonders if it will kill her to put everything up for sale. The boyfriend, for his part, is whiter than white, and his fingertips are cold. At times, they move as if sketching the outline of small shallow lagoons. And hills too soft to the touch. He used to tell Alice about his cleft palate corrected long ago by a specialist with eyes so deadened that they traumatized him for years. She's reminded of the deformity whenever his jaw quivers from too much intimacy, the possibility of being totally erased. Could there be such a thing? she wonders.

Neither Alice nor he comes on time, but with practice they could form a train. She wonders if success could come from dancing fingers and half-steps. They dress, and at the door, she whispers goodbye, see you tomorrow or the next day. Banalsounding, yet the innuendos are deeper than their favorite sitcoms. She thinks of two hobo souls in love and how much longer before they kill themselves with free-flowing emptiness. There's a stirring from the mother's room.

Alice returns to her apartment and sits on the bed. She thinks of the mother and how the two of them might be adrift in a circular sea. The mother who raised her son alone in a neighborhood of grifters and numbed veterans of some war or another. Alice wants to tell the wall that she still feels nothing, or that she's afraid to feel anything. To be hurt, she would have to die again, and before being reborn as a new Alice, she would have to become her own ghost. To tread the world without touching anything. It's happened so many times. She feels too old to melt or solidify.

By morning, the sun will rise unexplained. Alice will talk to no one. She thinks of how the boyfriend will keep trying to impregnate her with his love of shadows and thin mists and possible treasures. There will be no paper trails.

Kyle Hemmings has work published in *Cherry Tree*, *Inch*, *Wigleaf*, *Unbroken Journal*, and elsewhere. His latest collection of text and art is *Amnesiacs of Summer* published by Yavanika Press. He loves street photography, 50s sci-fi flicks, and obscure 60s garage bands.

POLAROID SNAPSHOT: SKINNY DIPPING IN THE LITTLE JUNIATA RIVER

PATRICK THOMAS HENRY

We thought the place where the cattails thinned was still the shallows, but the water came up to the inverted "V" where your ribs fused together. The Xiphoid process—a name I cannot forget, an extraterrestrial name for a bit of ossified cartilage that welds the ribs into a cage. The moonlight beamed upon the stream, a silvery light seen only in B-movie abductions. In the faded still shot, your backlit torso had already dematerialized, a silhouette where a body ought to have been. On the water your torso's twin, a water-severed reflection, surrendered to the mercury-white column of light. A tractor beam, drawing you from us. That's no moon, we heard you say. It's a trap! (Would you scream that, those months later, when your Humvee raged over the packed earth toward what you thought was a dry-rotted beam?) Your muscles didn't ripple that night but the water did. Abductee's terror, apostolic rapture: whatever you felt, it compelled you to raise your hands above your head. The cattails' wands raked the water; they were brown-black as sticks left in the fire ring, charred as the remnants of afterburners kicking a vessel into the stratosphere. From one of your hands, creek water sieved in silver grains. We know it can't be so, but even then we thought each drop struck the water and sizzled like molten fragments of shrapnel.

Patrick Thomas Henry is the fiction and poetry editor for *Modern Language Studies*. His work has appeared in *CHEAP POP*, *Passages North*, *Longleaf Review*, *Clarion*, and the *Massachusetts Review*, amongst others. He teaches creative writing at the University of North Dakota. Find him online at patrick-thomashenry.com and on Twitter @Patrick_T_Henry

DOWN THE LONG, LONG LINE

MARY-JANE HOLMES

Dark to light, the tunnel births the train and there's the river's head damned blue to reservoir, the ore rakes Da hushed lead from since the valley was drowned, the best sward spoiled, there's the clough where Ma netted sparrow (Spuggy, Sprog, Squidgie, Sparky) for a farthing a brace, there's the old hall where you went into service, steaming, pressing, goffering; lye burning the skin off your fingers, there's the hunting lodge where the master took you, holding his hand against your mouth while outside they beat and flushed grouse, there's the ginnel at the backend of town where they said you could be pure again: tansy oil, pennyroyal, rue, ergot, opium. There are the sidings where you lay wishing the wheels would roll away your shame, there's the train station where you marched the rails with the other girls: Lytton, Pankhurst, Kenney, Dunlop with axe, stones and a message. *Deeds not Words*. There's the prison they put you in, there's the gag they prised open your jaw with, the tube they force fed you with, there is the spit you lobbied back, there's the polling card, the pen in your hand, there's the river's mouth cleaned up enough that fish (ealpout, cod, whiting, smelt) have taken to spawning again.

Mary-Jane Holmes is an Anglo-Irish writer based in the Durham Dales, UK. She's been published in such places as *The Best Small Fictions Anthology* 2016 & 2018, *The Journal of Compressed Creative Arts*, *Spelk*, *Cabinet of Heed*, *FlashBack Fiction*, *The Lonely Crowd*, *Mslexia* and *Prole*, amongst others. www.mary-janeholmes.com

FLAT STANLEY GRABS A BURRITO

JENNIFER HOWARD

for lunch and cleans his toilet and pulls into gas stations and spends time in the mundane just like you do, but he also stumbled on a beaver dam on his walk in the woods and watched a sailboat corner the Black Rocks out on Lake Superior and a tiny neon blue bug landed on his paper finger while he was on the porch. When he is surrounded by concrete and plastic and car horns, Flat Stanley can perhaps imagine why people murder other people but there are always maple trees transforming themselves yellow, and goofy fish, and snowflakes! So many serial killers practiced in beautiful parts of the country: the icy forests of Alaska, and in Florida, so full of sunshine and alligators. Even a sky shifting at dusk over the ugliest parking lot becomes glory, inspires Flat Stanley to text a person he loves them. He will soon hop onto a plane heading toward that person, in Spokane, where Robert Lee Yates shot at least 13 women in the head and buried them in woods so pretty the women would have surely written poems if left alive and given notebooks.

Jennifer A. Howard teaches and edits *Passages North* in Michigan's snowy Upper Peninsula. Her collection of flash sci-fi, *You on Mars*, was published by The Cupboard Pamphlet.

SKYSCRAPER WOMAN

EMMA HUTTON

Your moon face in the box is the realest unreal thing that I have ever seen. Cheeks stamped pink. Bones bolted back together. In a dress you could only ever be seen dead in. I lean over for a closer look, hold onto the oak-lined edges and let my insides make new shapes.

"Let's go," you said, before the start of the three-legged race. We ducked past the prefects and walked to the gallery that looks like a factory. You wanted to see the sculpture of the man-eating snake but it wasn't there. We sat in a room full of paintings of skyscraper women all flecked with gold. You dared me to kiss the one with pink lips and orange hair. I shook my head. You smiled like a clown with a pickaxe, drew a red ring around your mouth. Then your lips were on her lips and my ears popped. A man in black screamed. A woman too. You dragged me out and over the wonky bridge and we ran until our cheeks burst vessels. You said the skyscraper woman tasted like wet leaves and chemistry. I pushed you against a wall and put my lips on yours. You tasted like big white flowers full of sun.

Pop.

Pop.

Pop.

I went away to learn things and when I came back you were gone. You didn't like the noises phones made so we wrote letters. I fell in love with a fat electrician. He asked about you. What you were like. The colour of your hair. The colour of your eyes. As if those were the things that mattered. I said you were the hiss of an orange. The open-eyed sting of the white-tiled underwater blue. I said you were made of gold.

You stayed away. Low to the ground, moving quickly, turning across the world.

After they pulled the baby out of me you sent a card— "To my favourite maker of death"—and I split my stitches. Pop, pop, pop.

My phone rang in the dark. Too early. Too late.

"Committed," they said. Died by, I thought.

"Jumped," they said. Dove, I thought.

Burst vessels.

Moon face, cold against my cheek. You taste like wet leaves and chemistry. Skyscraper woman, broken apart against the rocks. The hiss and sting of you wedged forever in me. Your lips the reddest red that I have ever seen.

Emma Hutton is an Irish writer based in London. Her stories have appeared in *The Mechanics' Institute Review*, *Litro* and *Southword*. She won the Mairtín Crawford Short Story Award 2019 and the TSS Flash Fiction 400 competition in spring 2019.

IN MY DREAM I SEE MY SON

JASON JACKSON

In my dream I see my son, and he's older, older, almost old, waiting for me to die. We're nothing like ourselves in a hospital room with a bed and a window looking out onto whiteness. There's a silence, a weight, which is difficult to shake. I can't speak, although I try, and my son can't hear, doesn't look at me, is bored, tired, sad, but also not quite there.

He won't remember enough of me, doesn't know who I really am, or was, or wanted to be, and as I try to whisper into the antiseptic silence I remember my own father. On the day he left the factory, he looked up to the sky and screamed. He didn't stop until a man called Frank took him by the shoulder and led him to The Crown where he sat and drank in silence, and he would not move until my mother came to take him home.

On his sixtieth birthday he went to a tattoo parlour and came out with the words *live without dead time* inked into his right forearm. He never gave a word of explanation to anyone.

So, from my dream-bed I tell my son—thirty years older than the boy he is today—*in your retelling of me, you'll be mistaken.*

And I think of what dies with me: the birdsong of the morning I arrived in a concrete Polish town; the thin, high clouds of Andalusia which made me weep for distance; how I sat and watched the fireworks at the end of the world with the woman who became my wife for a while, how we survived, then fell apart. The elephant that winked at me. The high tree I couldn't climb. The goal—all the goals—and the strings of my guitar.

There are boxed-up words he'll burn, because who would want to know? And the women, and the sex, and the blood in the dark, the sing-song, bed-breaking, coughed-up, coupled-up, sink-staining, sheet-stinking, red-white-and-black of it all.

These private worlds and these worries of age. The four-in-the-mornings which unmade me, which made me what I am.

When I wake from this dream I'll go quickly to his room, and I'll hold him the way my father held me.

Jason Jackson's prize-winning fiction appears regularly in print and online. Recent publications include *The Nottingham Review*, *New Flash Fiction Review* and *Spelk*. Jason is also a photographer, and his prose/photography hybrid work *The Unit* is published by A3 Press. Jason tweets regularly @jj_fiction

GIANTS

STEVEN JOHN

For you, the best part of our honeymoon was the Giant Tortoises. You'd collect lettuce leaves off the hotel's buffet table in your handbag then go to the tropical gardens that surrounded our bedroom veranda. You'd feed the tortoise's Neanderthal faces and stroke the warm mahogany houses on their backs, as if they could feel your pale, delicate hands.

For me, the best part of our honeymoon was winning on the roulette table the night we arrived. I put a hundred on number 10—the date we got married. Won enough to pay for the trip. Then, over the next three nights, you sat beside me at the tables, head on my shoulder, turning to the light the jewel I'd put on your finger. And I turned you to the light, for other men to wonder at. I lost every penny.

We'd drink pink wine at lunchtime in the heat of the sun then go back to our room. We didn't have much to pull off each other—a bikini, a pair of swim shorts. You'd fondle between my legs and say that it reminded you of a tortoise's neck and head. All it needed was a grasping mouth. I'd walk into the bedroom from the shower and see your form on the huge white bed, the mosquito nets blurring your breasts and limbs, your face turned to the open window. The giant tortoises were calling. Their sad, low pitched mating groans that shook the foundations.

Steven John's writing has appeared in *Burningword*, *Bending Genres*, *Spelk*, *Ellipsis Zine* and *Best Microfiction 2019*, amongst others. He's won Ad Hoc Fiction a record seven times and been nominated for a BIFFY award and the Pushcart Prize. Steven lives in The Cotswolds, England, and is Fiction Editor at *New Flash Fiction Review*.

KISS ME, KISS ME, KISS ME (1987)

JOSHUA JONES

Let them say I'm queer. (I'm not.) Let them taunt my stride, my accent, the songs I listen to. My hair sprayed so high. They already think I wear makeup. (So what if next year, in college, I'll think about kissing Jonathan, beautiful Jonathan, who'll have red lips just like mine.) Let them say whatever. (An erection during that homoerotic Japanese film will mean nothing.) I have a girlfriend (sort of). Gotten to second base (I think). She even talked blowjobs with me. (And those times in the Blockbuster stock room 15 years from now won't count—him married, me engaged. Besides, my fiancée will have Netflix by then.) *Gotta relax your throat*, my girlfriend said and held my hand. This was after youth group, in the back of her mom's Astro van, the tape deck blaring "Just Like Heaven." Now she kohls my eyes and asks which lipstick I want. *Bright red*, I say. *The brightest you've got.* Side B plays "Icing Sugar" as the stick glides across my mouth, a smeary streak like Robert Smith's kiss. Across my cheeks like the fiercest warpaint.

Joshua Jones' writing has appeared or is forthcoming in *The Best Small Fictions 2019*, *The Cincinnati Review*, *CRAFT*, *Juked*, *matchbook*, *Paper Darts*, *SmokeLong Quarterly*, *Split Lip*, and elsewhere. He lives in Maryland.

THE DAY THE BIRDS CAME

KYRA KONDIS

At first, there was just one: a scarlet macaw. It followed Patricia onto the school bus, nipped at the pink-plastic butterfly clips holding back her bangs, dug its talons into her bag. We asked Patricia, *What's with the bird?* and she shrugged and turned magenta and looked at her knees. When the bus driver tried to shoo it away, it smacked him in the face with its big crimson wings, and we all wondered why cool stuff like that didn't happen to us.

At lunch, four more appeared. Two goldfinches, a pigeon, and a Canada goose. The goose honked after Patricia as she carried her tray to her table. The pigeon pecked the corn out of her succotash. We whispered, *Why Patricia? What does she have that we don't?* and Patricia poked at her food, gingerly shuttling bites to her mouth while the birds pricked her hands with their beaks.

In math class, there were even more—birds we didn't know the name of, birds that perched on Patricia's shoulders, birds that fluffed up their wings and squawked her name into the stuffy classroom air. Patricia hunched down in her seat until Mr. Bollinger excused her from class, and we all wondered how,

how, *how* anyone could get so lucky.

By three, there were so many, we couldn't keep track of them anymore. While we waited for the bus, some of them hovered around Patricia like a cloud of crayon-box colors, and the rest weighed down the crabapple tree by the playground, the telephone wire, the rungs of the jungle gym. If one more bird landed there, even just a small one, we thought it might be enough to sink the whole world down lower in the sky, and that felt important. We wished we were important like Patricia; we wished we had whatever it was that she did.

And then, there was no more Patricia—there were just birds. Birds flitting home because they were too big for the bus. Birds, we imagined, waddling around Patricia's living room, nibbling on her textbooks, eating her unwanted vegetables. *She's so lucky,* we whispered to ourselves as we sprinkled birdseed on our windows that night, as we filled our backpacks with Ziploc bags of worms, as we doodled wings on our math homework. *She's so lucky, she's so interesting, she's so cool.*

Kyra Kondis is an MFA candidate in fiction at George Mason University, where she is also the assistant editor-in-chief of *So to Speak Journal*. She has been published in *Pithead Chapel*, *Wigleaf*, *Necessary Fiction*, and other wonderful places, and was a finalist in the 2019 *Lascaux Review* flash fiction contest.

WARSAW CIRCUS

KATHRYN KULPA

Our timing is perfect, a three-minute distraction.

We pass, we flirt, I drop a handkerchief; he bends to retrieve it (the sway of his exaggerated bottom! The laughter!); the return, the curtsey, the bow; our dance, a farcical mazurka, faces pushed close together, bodies angled out; he produces from one of his innumerable pockets a rose; we kiss.

Josef's face is so close to mine I can smell the greasepaint, see where sweat has left tunnels like tears. His plastered makeup smells like egg whites, that shiny gloss stage, when you're done beating and ready to bake.

Or maybe it just looks like egg whites, and I imagine the smell. I remember bakery windows full of tiny iced cakes in every color, pillowy loaves of challah, crusty boulders of rye. I remember when anyone could buy eggs and sugar. Could buy a train ticket and go wherever they liked.

Marta is good as gold through the whole act, not a poke, not a peep. I sewed the harness in Josef's costume, showed her how to fold in her arms and legs, tuck her head between her shoulders. Like doing a somersault, I said. She's watched the tumblers; she knows.

Curled up in her harness, quiet as a rabbit, she knows. But no one else knows. She disappears. They see a clown with a huge, padded bottom, a ridiculous fat figure swaying and dancing his clumsy dance, and everyone laughs. They don't see Marta.

You were good, I tell her after. Everybody clapped!

May she be so good when we cross the border.

HISTORIC PRESERVATION

KATHRYN KULPA

Mornings, the steep stone stairs grow steeper every day. The musty smell of locked rooms. Burnt-on muck at the bottom of the coffee pot that nobody cleans. But mornings are calls, appointments, applications to review; your fingers fly. It's the hours after lunch that make you think about cell death. There's a word for it, you looked it up: apoptosis. All those neurons, fizzing and popping. Life out of balance. Your life as a resource that cannot be renewed. Late afternoons, when the smell of cigarette smoke seeps through the walls, thick and grey and granite, but not thick enough to keep out the press of poverty. The brown ceiling stain that grows day after dull damp day, as if anyone could fight the rain and win. Whoever said *safe as houses* never played, as a child, in an abandoned house, never felt their foot break through rotted wood; never held tight to splintered floorboards, not feeling until hours later the 18 shards of wood dug from your fingers by a sewing needle in a mother's patient hands; feeling only the dangling weight of your legs, searching in air; the two friends who ran for help, the one who

stayed, counting with you, *one Mississippi*, *two;*
never dreaming of a time when hanging on every
day would scare you more than falling.

WHY I GOT WRITTEN UP BY THE MANAGER AT UNCLE EARL'S WORLD-FAMOUS BAR-B-Q

KATHRYN KULPA

Smother me in redneck kisses. Pour that smoky Bar-B-Q down my neck and lick it off, no rush. Time disappears, I'm boneless, honey-glazed, on fire in the walk-in freezer. We breathe in the popsicle air, so attuned, knocking over packages of hand-cut fries, nobody's hand cut those fries, they're damned crinkle cuts, people can be so stupid, like we're stupid now. I let him walk out before me. Brandon's bitching about the line, no such thing as a smoke break, and did I bring the key lime pie?

I tug my bra straps back up, say: We're out of pie.

Kathryn Kulpa is a writer and editor with work published in *JMWW*, *Pithead Chapel*, *Smokelong Quarterly*, *Women's Studies Quarterly*, and other journals. She was a winner of the Vella Chapbook Contest for her flash chapbook *Girls on Film*. She was born in a small state, and she writes short stories.

JUMPER

SARAH LAYDEN

Our small screens replayed the moment when the student leapt from the campus center balcony. We were there but witnessed nothing. We were training our tiny cameras to see the blue sky dotted by a line of towers; the hot-dog-eating contest in the food court; the spaghetti-sauce splatters (again) in the employee break-room microwave; the patients out the window walking slow to the cancer hospital, slow from the cancer hospital, one smoking a cigarette around an oxygen mask. We were spies in plain sight, watching each other online, noticing the ex now watching someone new. We checked our teeth and hair and nostrils in the reflections of our phones. We turned the bathroom into a hall of mirrors, gilt tarnished, a line of selves, stretching in opposite directions, with a single face. One of us was recording a song and caught the jumper in the frame. The video made the local news and logged more views than the politician who was caught doing—what had he done? That was weeks ago, or maybe months. The singer didn't miss a note; days later she signed her first record contract. Now we are watching the jumper video and asking how on earth we missed it. We were *right there*. Later, we felt as if we'd missed nothing. We'd caught and cradled the moment on our hard drives and caressed the buttons to make the video replay on a loop. We were there. I was. He wasn't my student. It wasn't like I knew him. With each viewing I am drawn to the lock of my own hair, wind-lifted, that appears to wrap the falling man in a hug. I say *man*, but I mean *boy*. I say *hair*, but I mean *noose*. Then the wind dies, the wind drops, the wind does everything it is supposed to do, because it is the wind. This can't be changed. Paused at the right moment, the jumper hovers, eyes open and staring into the lens, without judgement. His being a premonition of stillness. Fixed, immutable. The play button is an arrow pointing to a distance we can't see or know or cross. Our fingers itch with the pushing.

Sarah Layden is the author of a novel, *Trip Through Your Wires*, and *The Story I Tell Myself About Myself*, winner of the Sonder Press Chapbook Competition. Her short fiction appears in *Boston Review*, *Blackbird*, *PANK*, *Moon City Review*, and elsewhere. She teaches creative writing at Indiana University-Purdue University Indianapolis.

TODDY'S GOT LICE AGAIN

TUCKER LEIGHTY-PHILLIPS

This is what I tell myself: she'll grow out of it, she's just a kid, it's part of being a parent. This is what I say regarding Toddy, who loves her lice like family. When she's without them, she acts like she's missing a teddy bear or her own birthday party. She rolls in grass the way a dog covers itself in stink, wiggling and twisting until her head becomes a floating hairy hive. You've got to see it. She'll find them in her sideburns, press her middle finger against her skin to trap the creatures, and rather than pinching them out, she'll push them further in, like she's collecting a child strayed too far from the house. Of course, the neighbor kids don't want to get near her, and the school's sent a stack of letters telling us to take care of the situation before she's expelled, and sleepovers at the house aren't possible because our place may as well be haunted. But the kid's happy. She talks to them, admires them being so close to her head and thoughts—likes knowing they can hear her secrets. As for me, I'm coping as best I can. Just feels like too many summer days are spent with Toddy's hair styled up with mayonnaise, trying to scare the buggers off for good, knowing it's useless because I can't trust her not to swan dive back into the tall grass, ostrich her head in the milkweed, tumble into nature a little too sacrificially.

Maybe it was my fault. We were poor. The proper treatment was expensive, she got used to the itching and scratching and bugs bouncing from shoulder to scalp. Maybe she found it easier to come home to a pillow springing with small black fireworks, a towel covered in dead like a battlefield, a car seat reminding us these things travel wherever we go. Maybe she just got used to it. That's what we do as humans, right? We find ways to turn our consequences into comforts, to say *maybe this is good enough, maybe this is what I deserve.*

Tucker Leighty-Phillips is a student and writer living in Tempe, Arizona. His social media is @TheNurtureBoy and his website is TuckerLP.net

JUST TO SAY

NATHAN ALLING LONG

dedicated to Raasa Leela De Montebello

Last week I meditated in a cabin in the woods beside a pear tree that fruited only two pears, or—I laughed when I thought of it—one pair.

The third step of my childhood home was cracked and weak, which is how, and when, I learned to walk carefully around things in the world.

Every day, I'd sit, then walk, sit, then walk, my mind focused on my body, my posture, my breath, and on those two ripening pears.

I was often sick as a child, and once, after a string of ailments, my doctor gave me a silver dollar, which made me feel so special, I recovered the next day.

A pear tree in the woods struck me as a rare thing.

The steps to the cabin were new and made not a sound.

On the last day of the retreat, I climbed the steps, reached out and held one of the pears in my hand, the weight of the thing, trying to distinguish the line that separated its skin from mine.

As a teenager, I liked to swim naked in the lake near our house, my body dissolving into the cold water.

A pear is not like a coin: it will not last but can be safely swallowed.

When I was six, I stole an apple from the neighbor's yard.

Despite a week of meditation, I stole that pear.

The owners of the cabin will know it was me ... unless they believe a squirrel or a bird took the pear.

I set the pear on my desk at home and stared at its solitude.

In the cabin, I became pure observation: a bird lighting from a branch, a squirrel rustling up a trunk, a cloud drifting above the trees.

I slept, dreaming of a forest becoming a staircase into nothingness and I woke to the pear staring at me like a question.

In meditation, one starts to see that the self is an illusion, that there is nothing there behind the story of "I".

I took the pear in my hand and took a bite.

In my fourth-grade cafeteria hung a poster that said, You Are What You Eat.

As I took each crisp bite, I said to myself, *This is what I am.*

Stolen fruit tastes sweeter—and more complicated.

To say you are sorry is to say you experienced pleasure and now guilt.

The pear, its sweet juice and pulp, its sharp stem and bitter seeds, is now a part of me.

I might well have been a bird or a squirrel, whom we never expect to say are sorry.

Now, alone in my room, what I feel is not a sorrow for what I have taken and eaten, but for the pear I left behind, the one that hangs from a branch, alone.

Nathan Alling Long's work appears in over 120 publications. Their flash collection, *The Origin of Doubt*, was a 2019 Lambda Literary Award finalist. The recipient of a Truman Capote fellowship, Bread Loaf and Sewanee Writers Conference scholarships, and three Pushcart nominations, Nathan lives in Philadelphia and teaches at Stockton University.

SETTLED

ALICE MAGLIO

I have six chairs. Three I trust, and three I question. I acquired them from Craigslist a couple years back. I met the chairs' original owner in the personals section: man seeking woman was his big opener. At the time I was in the market for something nondescript. We fucked, and he looked at me a little, looked mostly at the wall. We didn't talk much. When it was over he smiled then turned to reassemble himself. As we walked out into the living room, he motioned to a set of dining chairs stranded in the far corner of the room. They were arranged in a rectangle with space in the middle for a table, but there was no table. What happened to the table? I asked. He shrugged languidly and looked at me as if I should understand. You need any chairs? he asked. I gave him two twenties, and he helped me load them into my car.

At home I discovered the chairs were of varying degrees of stability. I dug out my screw driver and did my best to tighten what was loose. Some holes were stripped and had no chance of recovery.

I bought a table. I felt better about the whole thing.

Alice Maglio's work has appeared in *Cosmonauts Avenue*, *Black Warrior Review*, *DIAGRAM*, *The Rupture*, *Wigleaf*, and *Gone Lawn*. She lives in New York and holds an MFA from Sarah Lawrence College.

STILL LIFE WITH PRAIRIE, 1860

NATALIE TEAL MCALLISTER

Line the little crosses outside Mother's window so she can see them. Little boys wander. Little boys play soldiers. Little boys play Indians. Tuck their little bodies into the earth where Mother can watch them grow.

Father makes the boxes and Mother makes the burial gowns. Ruby watches her mother dress the little baby boys and cradle them and they are almost real, more real than Ruby or the sunflowers or the sky. Mother pulls them into her chest and smiles while she rocks them. They belong to the crook of her arm.

Would Ruby like to hold the baby?

Father pulls Ruby back with his too-large hands. Little baby boys make no sounds. Little baby boys won't be warm. Little baby boys blue like the sky above.

Father lets Mother keep each boy until the sun sets.

At dusk Father cleaves the boys from Mother's arms. Into the box. Into the belly of the earth. Sky above turned turquoise and fuchsia.

Summer, harvest, pin oak leaves and frost. Six is arriving. Father plunges the shovel while Mother screams. His boys are made for earth, his only girl made to bear the weight of them.

Would Ruby like to hold the baby?

Yes, yes, mama I want to hold the baby.

Pull the baby in close. Hold the head in the nook of her arm. Arms as stiff as her baby doll. Legs as stiff as her baby doll. Tilt him forward. Open, eyes, open.

The hills curl around them. Father makes the box and Mother makes the burial gown. Ruby rocks the baby and rocks the baby and rocks the baby. Father cleaves the boy from her arms.

Snow, frozen earth, cracks in the hard clay. Father packs his rifle. Father packs his boots. Fire floats along the border. Boys ride horses to the flames. Boys belong to causes. Boys belong to armies.

Thaw, charred timber, mud sucks at their boots. The boys return in boxes.

Mother knows the price of boys and when their house burns Mother will teach Ruby how to build it again and build it stronger.

Ruby lets coneflowers grow along the little crosses.

Purple as the sky. Little girls be brave, brave as your mother. Little boys be meant for the earth, let your blood water the prairie and come alive again in the red of sunset.

Natalie Teal McAllister is a fiction writer by night, marketing director by day, based in Kansas City. Her short fiction appears in *Glimmer Train*, *No Tokens*, *Pigeon Pages*, *Midwestern Gothic*, *Craft*, and *SmokeLong Quarterly*, among others. Natalie spends her writing hours engulfed in several novels and assorted strange stories.

DIRTY MOUTH

FRANKIE MCMILLAN

I could always tell when the soap woman had been to our house. For one thing, my father appeared brighter and when he spoke it was proper and clean and not about shite hole, scumbag, tommy rotter and up your coozie. *What other clues were there?*

A faint smell left on the kettle, around the teacup where her soap hand had been.

She ought to cut that soap hand off, I told my father.

My father smoothed down his hair. He eyed himself in the mirror. "Don't go getting yourself in a lather, it's only cleaning she does."

Ah, but I knew otherwise. I'd seen her crouching down at the cabinet maker's workshop. Her skirts tied up at her waist, her lardy thighs on show. Running her slippery hand over the runners of drawers to make them slide easy. I'd seen her wrap her hand around a screw before drilling it in place, seen her slide her smeary fingers inside a shoe to soften the heel, sigh as her hand slipped inside a man's leather coat.

And now she was banging on our door again with

her pale lumpen hand.

"Is your Ma in?" She swung her tin bucket in front of her. "Only I'm not staying long."

So typical I thought. Full of slither and slather and quick down the gurgler she goes.

"Don't be daft," I said. This is what Ma would have said and the words came easy. Behind me I could hear my father cursing about the terrible situation in the bathroom. I knew it was a ruse. They'd lock themselves in there. My father and the soap woman. She'd sit on his knee, lick his earlobes, wash his mouth out with that big creamy hand of hers. Later he would emerge, bright eyed and whistling as if to throw us off the scent.

THE FISH MY FATHER GAVE ME

FRANKIE MCMILLAN

I drowned the fish even though I knew I was too old to be drowning a fish. It was as big as a real fish and I let it float for a while. My father stared into the bathtub. "Sweet Jaysus," he cried, "did your mother teach you that?"

My father was a drunk, a dream, a chaser of women, a storyteller, he came from the Irish bog, his hat was riddled with bullet holes, he cried on Easter Sunday, got down on his hands and knees to look at a hedgehog, danced with my mother, smashed the shop window then stumbled home with a chocolate fish. "You shall have a fishy on a little dishy," he sang, opening his mouth so wide you could see the gleam of his gold tooth.

I cannot write about my father or if I do the story meanders, twists away from me in a slither. How can you nail a father down? Every goodbye was a wink and "I'll come back with something for ye!"

The fish felt heavy in my palm. I traced my fingers over the ripples of chocolate skin, from the tail to the blunted snout. My father stood there, pleased with himself.

To drown a fish takes time. It tries to change shape, squeeze through your fingers. It muddies the bath water. It gets your parents talking.

THE STORY INSIDE HER

FRANKIE MCMILLAN

There is a story inside her and it is about a story running for its life and in the story there are riflemen in blue breeches who cock their muskets and take aim. FIRE shouts the captain. Gunpowder blasts the seat of the story's pants but the story keeps running over the marshy ground. All around other stories are running, dodging this way and that. Some stories fall like dying swans. Somewhere in the story she sees blasted feathers, and from a tree, a dangling participle. Where is the white flag in this story? Where are the stretcher boys to rescue the story? But oh, look—the story, the story that started it all keeps running. Now there are only ten of them left and the border is in sight. Hooray they cry to each other. Hooray, keep going!

The story inside her says, that is your ending. But the story running for its life has its own ideas. The Captain must come back. He must tweak his magnificent moustache and declare something wise like, 'Do not hide your light under a bushel.' But who knows what a bushel is? Not the story running and not the little story inside her which is beginning to think that maybe that's where the story should safely remain.

Frankie McMillan is the author of five books, the most recent of which, *The Father of Octopus Wrestling and other small fictions*, was listed by Spinoff as one of the ten best NZ fiction books of 2019. She has won numerous awards and residencies including the NZSA Peter and Dianne Beatson Fellowship, 2019.

FOR TWO BLUE LINES

HEMA NATARAJU

Yesterday it was strawberries. Today, it's dirt.

After Sanjay leaves for work, I breathe easy. There's an overgrown rose bush in my backyard garden. I kneel beside it, submit myself to that shrine. With my bare hands, I dig at the roots, tearing open the layer of hard, cracked mud until I reach the soft, damp earth beneath. I grab clumps of it and squish it in my palms, trying to squeeze the fertility out of it, and put it in my mouth.

It tastes of generations of rose plants, of mothers and daughters who flowered and withered and flowered again.

The sun warms my head in blessing. In that moment, loneliness stops gnawing under my skin. I'm understood. I'm free. Two mynah birds flit around me. *One for sorrow, two for joy...*

I've stifled this feeling for Sanjay, but now hope soars in my chest like an untethered helium balloon.

I go inside and bring out a little notebook that I've hidden in the rice barrel. "Dirt" is last in the list of pregnancy cravings of women, of mothers in my family.

I check it off and I hope, I pray, I beg for something to take root inside me.

Hema is an Indian-American writer living in Singapore with her husband and kids. Her most recent work has appeared in *MORIA Online*, *Spelk Fiction*, *The Brown Orient*, *National Flash Fiction Day*, and in a couple of print anthologies including *Chicken Soup for the Soul*. She tweets as @m_ixedbag.

BLOOM

KARI NGUYEN

Girl takes the yellow chalk from the cardboard box lying on its side in the shadow of the brick wall of the school. Beyond the large square of pavement she can see the backs of the officers visible through the chain fencing. They are spaced evenly, every few yards, facing forwards unless she is to yell, or make any other sound loud enough for them to hear her. Girl loves to draw, twirl, and also to yell at the officers, things in her native tongue which mean nothing much to them, just small person noise. They check on her by turning their heads, and then they turn back around. To them she is Girl and nothing more, no other name needed, or at least this is what she assumes because they don't ask her name, or give her theirs. When her turn is over in a few minutes' time the next one will also be Girl, and then Boy, Boy, and so on, until everyone has had their air.

With the chalk, Girl writes her name, Maitea, in a free space on the blacktop. They are allowed to write as long as the words aren't bad, and Maitea knows her name means love, or at least that's what her father told her when she'd climbed up into his lap so that he could detangle her hair with a comb that first morning after breakfast, after her mother had been called away.

She wonders how the others carry love, when it is not in their name. This bothers her, but she doesn't have the words in any language (yet) to begin exploring or making sense of these ideas.

A breeze kicks up and the few trees out along the road begin to stir. The chalk in her hand moves across the ground, bumpy and imperfect in its path. Maitea is drawing what looks to be a large teardrop outlined in yellow, which she then quickly shades, as there isn't much time left for her out here. She draws another, then another—out, arc, and back again, with a quick shade—many of them, scattered randomly across the tar where she can find room. They look like enormous drops of rain that have fallen sideways, tears of a giant or perhaps a God.

The wind nips at the shapes in chalk, and begins carefully lifting their edges, rippling them a little and then still more before loosening the entire shapes and spinning them into the air. Up, up they go. Maitea glances back at the teacher, who has opened the glass door and has a hand to her mouth. The teardrops begin to shuffle, and instead of falling back down they begin to join, to make way for each other, their tapered ends adhering together in the center of what is now a giant yellow flower—can you picture it spinning? The officers turn, some with guns raised, and one shouts, "Who did this?"

Maitea beams and shouts her name.

Kari Nguyen lives in New England with her husband, daughter, and twin sons. She writes fiction and nonfiction and is the former nonfiction editor for *Stymie* Magazine. Her stories are included in several recent anthologies including *America's Emerging Literary Fiction Writers: Northeast Region*. For more of her work, visit karinguyen.wordpress.com.

THIS IS A COMB

LEILA ORTIZ

This is the president tweeting. This is my fake, white tree. This is my name spelled correctly. Someone complemented me. Then I got dissed. There are ghosts slipping between my fingers. They are wringing their hands. I want to hole up in my place and never come out. I want to call my ex. Here are some bitches who think they're punk rock. When I say bitch it isn't gendered. This time. Here's a sock without a match. Here's a person who really doesn't care. Here's a person who wishes desperately to care, but most of all, to understand. This is someone showing me a poem. This is me feeling shame. When the poets talk I want to participate. Here I am trying to participate and exaggerating myself as a protective measure. It is still me, but performed. The realer me sneaks in: I'm getting pissed and trying to stay cordial. The ghosts are drying their hair. I am under water. I want to come up for air.

Leila Ortiz was born and raised in New York City, where she still lives. She is the author of two chapbooks, *Girl Life* (Recreation

League, 2016) and *A Mouth is Not a Place* (dancing girl press, 2017). Leila is a graduate of The Queens College MFA Program in Creative Writing and Literary Translation.

BRASS

MELISSA OSTROM

In the dim station, close to the tiled wall, among a press of harried people, near the clean passing chords of a saxophonist's bebop, Ruben had stared. Not at the woman, technically. He'd been admiring her coat. His mother had worn one exactly like it: a navy all-weather Count Romi from Neiman Marcus, with brass buttons, a bit of a buckle on each side of the waist, and pintucks that formed neat rows down the front. (And wasn't that how he remembered her—not at the end of her life but at the beginning of his? A knot of hair at her nape, the grip of her hand, and at the school door, the firm hug, his brow briefly branded with a button, and then her "Be good," the swift release, and a cloud of lemons and lilies. Chanel No. 5 stayed longer than she did.) He was sorry. He'd only toed up the hem to check the color of the lining. (And yes—just right—a satin-like crushed violets.) Truly, Officer.

Melissa Ostrom is an English teacher and the author of *The Beloved Wild* (Macmillan, 2018) and *Unleaving* (Macmillan,

2019). Her stories have appeared in several journals, and her flash "Ruinous Finality" was selected for *The Best Small Fictions 2019*. Learn more at www.melissaostrom.com or find Melissa on Twitter @melostrom.

PONDS

PAMELA PAINTER

This summer we're renting a cottage not in Maine, but in a new place on the outer Cape. And just like past summers, you'll pack your own suitcase, not the one with pajamas and shorts and swimsuits, but the pink suitcase with Ishbel, your fuzzy goat, and games, and books from your shelf. You will have a room all to yourself, mysteriously, and we'll make sure it is close to our room for when you call out in the night, which you have almost stopped doing. Yes, you can stay up as late as Danny used to—how do you remember that—and you won't have to think about the ocean. Tides and riptides are words we will not use. The kettle ponds are round and calm, home to tadpoles we will watch turn into frogs, and you will marvel about how things grow and change—like tadpoles and caterpillars—and be sad that some things don't.

Pamela Painter's flash collection is *Wouldn't You Like to Know*. Her stories appear in numerous journals, and in the anthologies *Sudden Fiction*, *Flash Fiction*, *Microfiction*, *New Micro* d *Nothing Short of 100*. Her collection, *Fabrications: New and Selected Stories* is due out from Johns Hopkins University Press in Fall 2020.

THE SUMMER HEAT FEELS JUST LIKE LOVE

JJ PEÑA

my friends are giggling & then laughing & then cackling in my apartment kitchen, each with cups of wine in hand, drinking as if to burn sins out of their bodies. one asks, *what would you title your life story right now?* an answer: WELL, I FUCKED THAT UP. another: WINNING AS A GOOGLY-EYED BITCH. & mine: HOW TO SURVIVE THE SUMMER WITHOUT AC. which makes everyone groan. there i go again, bitchin about the heat. yet none of them lives in an apartment that eats the day & throws it up at night. *stop complaining,* they say before i make a fuss. *we're children of the desert. you're supposed to be used to the heat.* this is true. pero like, being born in a desert & surviving in one are two separate things. they say: *remember our philosophy class? you just have to think of the heat in another way.* & i know they're referring to when we read aristotle. he believed we birthed tiny suns in our chests when we entered the world. not a crazy concept to buy into—to test his theory, all you have to do is put your palm to your heart to feel the fire we make. but that image won't make me any less hot at night or stop my dehydrating-insomnia, & i let them know that: *i'll think of that when i'm shoveling ice out of the freezer & throwing it onto my sheets.* not a response that goes over well. insert dramatic eye-rolls & stage-effect moans. *just be lucky*, one of my friends begins, *you're single. imagine how worse the night could be.* i don't tell them that's exactly what i daydream about before passing out because then i'd have to tell them what i imagine: the heat, finding love, which my sister describes as the colliding of two suns.

JJ Peña is a queer, burrito-blooded writer, living & existing in El Paso, Texas. His work appears in, or is forthcoming from, *Passages North*, *Cherry Tree*, *Five Points*, *Hayden's Ferry Review*, & elsewhere. He has an MFA from The University of Texas at El Paso.

WHEN YOU FIRST MEET THE TELEPATH

MEGHAN PHILLIPS

she tells you she can make you come without touching—make you come with her mind—& you tell her that's a hell of a line & buy her a beer anyway because she has a swimmer's shoulders & a black muscle tank & eyeliner so perfectly smudged that you're tempted to go home with her just so she'll do your eyes the next morning before sending you out to the gas station on the corner for coffees and Tastykakes & while you're already waking up in her bed tomorrow, she's still in tonight asking about your job at the library & the last book you read, knocking over your empties as she reaches to pop a quarter into the bar's tiny juke box, laughing as she pulls down the neck of her shirt to show the two dots tattooed on her collarbone—two pips for a lieutenant commander in Starfleet (like Geordi!)—you'll think this is what she means because you can feel your cheeks blooming & your heart stutter-stepping from the attention of this woman, so when you ask her only half embarrassed if this is how she'll make you come with her mind (because it's working, it's working) she shakes her head, touches your hand—may I?—& it's then that you feel her voice in your brain—"so much of pleasure is mental"—& she smiles over the rim of her glass & it feels like when you were a kid on your back in a field, the boom-crash of fireworks echoing in your chest & it feels like it's 10:30 on a Saturday night & you're driving the back roads of your home town, all corn fields & moonlight & your favorite song's on the radio & you're cresting one hill then another & another & she's smiling at you from the passenger seat & both of you are gone.

Meghan Phillips is a 2020 National Endowment for the Arts Literature Fellow. Her flash fiction chapbook *Abstinence Only* is forthcoming from Barrelhouse Books. Her stories have been anthologized in *Best Microfiction 2019* and *Best Small Fictions 2019*. She lives in Manheim, PA with her husband and son.

COMPENSATION

KEN POYNER

For some time now I have been dating confetti. The hardest part is finding places to go. If we go somewhere windy, most of our time is spent collecting all her windblown pieces, stopping afterward for cardboard paper and shears to make up for fragments that will never be seen again. The pool is a disaster. I keep a net in the car, and after swimming, I dry her out on the sidewalk or spread her over other warm pavement or on the hood of the car. Traditional dating options, like movies, are much better. I can sprinkle her across one seat, hope that no one brushing past picks up any stray pieces, that most of her lasts through the entire viewing.

Long hours of the morning are spent weighing and sorting and hoping we have ended our date with all the slivers of her that we started with. We remake what we miss, we recomb our environment, we agree there should be a little less of that, a little more of this. We evolve.

All my friends ask if she is worth the work—the loss and replenishment, the chasing lone loose pieces, the accounting for the collected whole of her. It is a relationship they cannot, at first, find value in. I let them imagine the balance sheet between us, the strange accounting that is our companionship.

Then I tell them of those special long, dry nights: a small room, or even a closet, the two of us widened and electric, accompanied by the enrapturing hum of one slowly, sensuously oscillating fan. Think. Think of her impishly streaming, uncultured, unformed, untethered, endless edges scurrying and improvident in the air.

Two of Ken Poyner's poetry collections and four of his short fiction collections are widely available. He lives with his power-lifter wife, various cats and betta fish in the southeastern corner of Virginia. He spent 33 years in information security, moonlighting as a writer. Now, he writes dangerously full-time.

DISSOLVE

SANTINO PRINZI

Unwrap the bath bomb, dip it into the steaming bath. Don't let it go. Don't let any of this go. Let the bubbles fizzle in your hand, let it dissolve through your fingertips. Hover your palm above the water. Gritty freshness catches beneath fingernails; you hope it never washes away. Count your breaths. Your eyes stream while you hold the bath bomb to your ears, ears once considered too small to hear sizzling. Step into the tub and smear the remnants of the bath bomb over your body, a body that's yours but not yours, a body you'll do something about soon, very soon. Action still overdue. Dry your eyes first, then the body. Your father thinks he knows what you're doing in there and he's only half right. He says, it ain't right for a man to spend so long in the bath. You don't correct his mis-gendering. He never listens. You sniff the air and smile. Six weeks until this humdrum town can fizzle through your fingers, until this man will deny all knowledge of your becoming. It all smells new like lemongrass and salt.

Santino Prinzi is a Co-Director of National Flash Fiction Day in the UK, and is one of the founding organisers of the annual Flash Fiction Festival. His flash fiction collection, *This Alone Could Save Us*, will be published in 2020 by Ad Hoc Fiction.

DOC HOLLIDAY GOES WEST

ALEYNA RENTZ

We're talking about the way life goes. The four
of us are sitting on floor pillows in Bella's studio
apartment, a little room right above the formalwear
store downtown, drinking cheap Moscato and
passing around a bag of pistachios. We're trying to
stay healthy, but we can only try so hard. This is
the way life goes: Bella's little sister got killed in
the shooting at Holliday High School two weeks
ago. It's named for Doc Holliday, a Georgia native
who moved out West to become a gunslinger. These
are the kind of school names you get in Georgia.
People are getting superstitious, sharing a Facebook
post that asks what anybody expected from a school
with a namesake like that. People are praying more
often. You see them in grocery store checkout lines,
eyes closed, lips working silently. Nobody touches
the tabloids anymore. There's no reason to look at
People when those same grieving mothers are all
around you, at the bank and the Dollar General
and purchasing family-sized buckets of dark meat
chicken from the KFC. Nobody cooks anymore, but
everyone's tired of casseroles. Bella's sister's in *US*

Weekly, one of the 15 dead featured on the cover. She was supposed to be a Broadway star, Bella tells us. She was rehearsing for this musical called *The Fantasticks* when someone pulled the fire alarm. She had a monologue at the beginning of the play about the wonders of being 16: *I like to touch my eyelids because they're never quite the same.* She had to stroke her face and spin circles around the stage, her skirt parachuting around her. She was supposed to fuckin' go places, Bella keeps telling us. We were all supposed to go places, but look where we are. Community college, office jobs. Before he'd draped his bedroom with flags from fallen regimes, the kid who shot up the school had been accepted to some tiny college up in the Blue Ridge Mountains on an ROTC scholarship. Before all the saloons and shoot-outs and the O.K. Corral, Doc Holliday was just a dentist. He told kids to floss more often. He stuck his hands in their mouths, told them to open wide.

Aleyna Rentz is a recent MFA graduate from Johns Hopkins University, where she currently teaches creative writing. Her work has appeared or is forthcoming in publications including *Glimmer Train*, *Pleiades*, *Fifth Wednesday*, *Passages North*, *Wigleaf*, and elsewhere. Currently, she serves as the senior fiction reader for *Salamander*.

HEARTWOOD

JOHANNA ROBINSON

I sit on the porch. There aren't many quiet moments like this. In our little village, there aren't many errands to run. The wood beneath my feet is old, the only part of the original house that is left; there are charred shadows in patches, and the black edges of the boards are lined and creviced like ancient knuckles, or lips. This ancient wood is greyer than the rest of the house, its rings harder. It's ten years, now, since we rebuilt the house. I'd watched Henrik fell the trees in the nearby woods. I'd marked each of them with a gash of red paint. I knew exactly which one the soldier had pushed me up against, which section of bark had scratched the skin between my shoulder blades, and the place either side of the trunk where my fingernails had dug into it. But I'd needed more than this one tree to go. All the others that I'd counted, back and forth, over the soldier's shoulder that thudded against mine, until it was over—they had to come down too. Henrik sliced open the trunks, roots to neck. He stripped the bark, split them over and over into planks, trimmed and sanded them until I was happy. Now they clad our bedroom, their grain like frozen waves. Henrik sanded them so well that when I lie in bed in the dark and pull my fingers across their surface, they feel like skin.

In the clearing, there are saplings.

Johanna began writing in 2016 and is now trying to make up for lost time. Her work features in *SmokeLong*, *Ellipsis Zine*, *Reflex Press* (where "Heartwood" won third place), and *Mslexia*. Her WWII novella-in-flash *Homing* is published by Ad Hoc Fiction and she is currently working on a historical novel-in-flash.

FERTILIZER

MICHELLE ROSS

When I was 17, men were always wanting to feed me. Steak, quiche, Big Macs, ice cream. They wanted to take me to restaurants, put stuff inside me. One man offered me chicken soup he'd made himself, and I swooned. I thought: this man truly cares for me. I ate that soup on his worn brown couch in front of his television. I don't remember what we watched, but I remember it was winter, the scratchy nubs of grass on his lawn frosted over. I remember I hadn't even finished that bowl of soup before he shucked my pants. I understood then the purpose of the soup: a garden won't feed you unless you feed it first. That man harvested all of me right there on the couch. I remember him telling me how good I tasted.

PALATE CLEANSER

MICHELLE ROSS

See this postcard of a hotel, this window circled in blue ink? That's the room in which I realized I would leave your father. You were there with me, in fact, though I'm sure you don't remember. You couldn't have been more than three. Your father was in Chicago for business, and on a whim, I drove us out of town for the weekend. I'd never done a thing like that in my life. Once we were settled into the hotel, I walked you down the street, a sidewalk shaded by enormous elms, ginkgos, and maples, to this French restaurant where they served a fixed menu every evening. Three courses, three choices per course. And in between the salad and the dessert: a palate cleanser. In this case, a lemon sorbet served in a little blue goblet. The grin on your face when the waiter set that blue goblet before you! Your own little goblet. For the courses, I had given you bites from my plate. You had eaten that food dutifully, but only the sorbet made you smile—before you even tasted it. Because it was beautiful. Because it was all yours. That's how I felt at that hotel. It was the first time in my life that I'd stayed at a hotel all by myself. Well, not by myself really. You were there. What I mean is I was the only adult. I was in charge. I could do whatever I wanted whenever I wanted. I could, for instance, take my toddler to a fancy restaurant that her father wouldn't even take me to. It was a feeling I hadn't known I was missing. And once I felt it, I wasn't willing to give it up. Like how after that palate cleanser, when the waiter brought out that one chocolate soufflé for us to share, your grin vanished. Your face reddened. The waiter had barely even taken his hand from the plate. I saw the look of panic on his face. You were the only child in the place, much less the only toddler. It was not the kind of restaurant where one took children. I quickly pushed that soufflé toward you before you wailed.

Michelle Ross is the author of *There's So Much They Haven't Told You* (2017), which won the 2016 Moon City Press Short Fiction Award. Her fiction has appeared in *Alaska Quarterly Review*, *Colorado Review*, *Electric Literature*, and other venues. She's fiction editor of *Atticus Review*.

CAUGHT

C.C. RUSSELL

You get caught because you have to write it all down. You get caught because of small discrepancies. When you aren't home when you said that you would be. You get caught in the simplest of ways. Because you are a walking cliché. Because of the text messages. When your phone keeps coming alive in the middle of the night. You get caught when you kiss him in the backroom where you work. Because you are smiling, touching your fingers to your lips. Because of your swagger. Because you telegraph it. You get caught when the skirt you come home in is different from the one that you left in. You get caught sitting in your car in the driveway. You get caught when trying to compose yourself in the hallway. You get caught because there are photos. Because there are messages undeleted. Because signs were left along the way. You get caught because your fingerprints are all over this. You get caught because you smell like him. Because you forgot to make the bed. You get caught when you aren't there. You get caught because you want to. You get caught. And it is this, the most satisfying bit of the whole affair.

C.C. Russell has published his poetry and prose in such journals as *The Meadow*, *New York Quarterly*, *The Colorado Review*, *Split Lip*, and *Whiskey Island*, among others. He lives in Wyoming with a couple of humans and several cats. You can find more of his work at ccrussell.net

FABLE TOLD FROM THE FUTURE WEST

AUSTIN SANCHEZ-MORAN

There was a man, who children in one-room class-rooms still learn about out west, who would go from town to town stealing all the old tubes of neon from cafes, pharmacies, and liquor store signs, then load them into his potato sack and move on. And the townspeople would storm from out of the backs of their stores, where they'd been sleeping or working on a greasy broken pipe, or something else that had suffered rust from neglect, and they'd see the old man's hair and his sack and they'd think, "There goes that Casey Jones, Johnny Appleseed, Davy Crockett of the neon alpenglow..."

It had been said that the old man had never made it to Las Vegas or even Reno. It's thought if he had made it there a little bit of his brains would drip out of his nose into his beard. No, he was strange enough. People claimed he lived off of only the fresh milk from cows, goats, and sheep that he'd collect in passing, without permission, on his way out of town. That's how he made it so well through the centuries.

But there was also an ending to the story that children never hear about. The man was actually on his way to dump all of the collected tubes into a gorge he'd been searching for all his life. And as legend has it, one day he got tired and dumped what he'd collected into a part of the Colorado that ran towards a waterfall. And as he fell back into the red sand, dead, all the lights came back on in the water's rolling current, and the river turned into a fluorescent milk that filled the gorge slowly. And today it shows up again, reflected down from the stars we sometimes see through the smog.

Austin Sanchez-Moran received his MFA in Poetry from George Mason University. His poems and short fiction have been published in *RHINO Poetry*, *Denver Quarterly*, and *Salamander Magazine*, among many others. He also had a poem chosen for the anthology, *Best New Poets of the Midwest* (2017). He is currently an English teacher at Choate Rosemary Hall in Connecticut.

SUMO WRESTLERS' HEATING SERVICE

ROBERT SCOTELLARO

During the harshest winters their phones are ringing off the hook. The chilling goosebumps that are rising as the north wind hurls its weight around. Loss-chilled women, willowy winter-bitten widows, all frozen stiff by life, by weather, by life's weather. The calls come in.

They always arrive in pairs at night. Their enormous heft through a doorway suddenly becoming smaller. An osmosis nearly, of fleshy immensity. Heating up the room at a glance. The sight of them.

A king-size bed is required as a precursor. There is an elaborate tea ceremony. They remove their clothes with a ritualistic poetry, an origami master's art for folding, till they are (in full and ample bulk) left in only their mawashi. They ease under the covers ironically like a whisper with only a bedsprings complaint. Positioning themselves, a belly-pointing sandwich of heat and comfort. Bookending a client, but not touching. An onionskin paper-thin margin between. The chills of winter withering for a time.

In the dark, a sweet song of Mt Fugi and the flapping of cranes overhead. Of lovers outside a red pagoda. And then later, alternating, first one reciting a haiku, softly in broken English and then the other, to oohs and aahs in the dark:

> The summer moon.
> There are a lot of paper lanterns
> on the street.

And then (as the cold wind falters against the window glass like an incompetent would-be intruder):

> The butterfly
> perfuming its wings
> fans the orchid ...

HIT MAN IN RETIREMENT

ROBERT SCOTELLARO

He awoke and dragged their bodies out of bed. He told himself it was the arthritis. Over coffee the voices were there (the usual suspects), some turning, startled, before a word could be uttered: the spray. Others begging—the big money offers, eyes bugged and jittery. One even offering his wife for a pass and a chance to leave the country.

But a job was a job, and what was a man if he couldn't do what he set out to do, be counted on. He glanced at the newspaper, some headlines, and shook his head with a *what's-the-world-coming-to* lopsided twist to his mouth. He looked forward to checking out the Obits.

There were some pigeons outside on the sill. They sounded like they were in love. He put out a few crumbs, but they fluttered off. They'd soon circle back. When he was younger he would have snapped their necks. He wondered if Janis would call. 32 years apart and he still liked a word or two. All those years she never asked questions.

He slow-walked back to the kitchen—dragged a

few bodies with him—their shoes scraping along the linoleum.

Robert Scotellaro is the author of seven literary chapbooks and four full-length collections of flash and microfiction. A fifth story collection is due out by Press 53, September 2020. Robert is also the co-editor of *New Micro: Exceptionally Short Fiction* (published by W. W. Norton, 2018). www.robertscotellaro.com

CUBISM

DARYL SCROGGINS

He broke from her; she watched him go—his things still there. Much later she saw him in another country. He asked about his stuff. She showed him photos of everything being carried away by strangers.

Daryl Scroggins is the author of *This Is Not the Way We Came In*, a collection of flash fiction and a flash novel (Ravenna Press). He lives in Marfa, Texas.

THE KITCHEN

CURTIS SMITH

The son cooks for his father. The old man's trailer.
Yellowed windows. Flies caught on dangling strips.
The son prepares meals for the week. The old man
smokes and pages through the magazines the son
has brought. The old man looks at the pictures,
reads a caption or two, turns the page. The son
makes shepherd's pie and chili. Last week, turkey
soup. A single meal eaten together, the rest refrigerated. As they eat, one of them will break the
silence and share a memory. A house they rented
along the railroad tracks, the locomotives' shaking
of windows and dishes. A creek where they fished
for steelheads and walleyes, the late summer's flow
speckled with milkweed seeds. A mutt named Bo.
The other man smiles. *Yes, I remember.* The son
has forgiven his father for his drinking. Forgiven
him for a childhood of chaos. This, to the son, is a
miracle, a revelation born from last fall's hospital
visit. The father wrinkled and broken. Tubes to
bring him oxygen and take his urine. The body the
boy had once feared now shriveled beneath an ill-
fitting gown. The son's forgiveness unplanned, a

145

reflex, and when the weight lifted, he was stunned by the lightness of his body. In the space where he'd once nurtured his hate there was now not love but an emptiness the son understood would be his to fill or ignore.

Later that evening, the son cooks with his daughter. On his clothes, the scent of his father's cigarettes. The little girl on a chair, a spatula in hand and an apron that reaches her ankles. The countertop a mess, but he doesn't scold her for the eggs she breaks or the flour she spills. Their kitchen so different, the sunlight and good smells. The girl talks, and he listens to it all, asking questions, feigning surprise. He won't let his daughter see her grandfather, but he brings pictures to the old man and tells him stories. The girl's fascination with creek-side frogs. The cat she dresses in dolls' clothes. The old man smiles. This is so new for all of them.

Curtis Smith's most recent books are *Beasts and Men* (stories, Press 53), *Kurt Vonnegut's Slaughterhouse-Five: Bookmarked* (cnf, Ig Publishing), and *Lovepain* (novel, Braddock Avenue Books). Later this year, Running Wild Press will release his next novel, *The Magpie's Return*.

MUSCLE

KAREN SMYTE

The summer I turned 16, I slept with my rowing coach. It was the first time I had sex in the way it happens sometimes, as a surprise. We were at his younger brother's funeral, my first boyfriend, then we were along the canal bank, on his suit jacket, me tightening my muscles around him.

Joe had his reasons, or didn't. He reminded me enough of Mike, straight angles everywhere, cheekbones, rib bones, hips sharp. I needed to stop the loop in my head of Mike loping to the dock, four blades on his shoulder, and the impossible grace he displayed setting them down.

I told Sue the next day. We walked to the hospital, past the convent where we played hide and seek as eight-year-olds. The main building stood empty now. Through the kitchen window we saw plates on a table collecting dust, harvesting mold, as if the nuns had left unexpectedly, as if they'd return. But there was no money to repair the plumbing and electricity, not from the Order, not from the city. Within a year the convent was leveled for the

Hawk Estates—only a brick fireplace inexplicably left standing near the new tennis courts.

At the emergency room, the doctor asked, not unkindly, why I hadn't used protection.

"I didn't think it'd get that far."

"Guess you need to be prepared for it to happen again," he said as he handed me six packs of birth control pills. "Two pills now, two more in twelve hours." As easy as that, if I took them soon, if there were no complications.

All that summer I ran three miles to the boathouse, then flung myself, no fear, against the oar during practice. My arms stretched out and reaching, quick with the hands, I'd drop my blade in and feel myself suspended against the weight of the water. My legs pushing. My body swinging back forcefully. My arms drawing in.

"You have such feel for the run of the boat," Joe said, but I was awed by the memory of my muscles, how they moved on their own.

Karen Smyte, a former Canadian National team rower and collegiate coach, is an educator living in Ann Arbor with her family. Chapters from her current novel-in-progress were performed at Selected Shorts at Symphony Space, published on *Electric Literature*, in *The Southampton Review*, *The Lascaux Review* and awarded a Bridport Prize.

EXIT MUSIC

BETH ANN SPENCER

Killing it, she was, just murdering the shit out of the funky keyboard we came across in an alley behind the Famous Musician's house. Always on the first of the month when the big double-duty dump truck hit his part of town we'd wander by after school to see what he was putting outside his back gate besides the Johnny Walker empties and, lately, a lot of Chivas. Rita knew lots of piano riffs by heart, and though of course the thing wasn't plugged in and was even missing one of the black keys in the middle—she hunched over and whaled on it until we could almost hear something we didn't know we'd been waiting for, something from Queen or, I don't know, Little Richard. Mitch and I were both in love with her and I wondered, watching her, whether he noticed the drop of sweat glistening above her lip or the tiniest edge of red bra flashing through the armhole of her t-shirt. A thing to remember about Rita was that she had been in group homes almost her whole life, until last year when her mom finally got out of jail and landed a job at Costco, so Rita was in general kind of an angry person, although less so the last few months. *Pump it up*, Mitch was singing, *until you can feel it*, and I thought for the millionth time how much better the old pissed-off Elvis Costello was than the married mellow man. On and on Rita played, some demon in her mind sending waves of rage out the ends of her fingers and the short, dyed dreads on her head. Like she was a sunspot, maybe, ready to explode and cause all the volcanoes on earth to erupt at once. In the few months we'd known her Rita had never given Mitch or me a single sign she wanted to be more than a friend, so neither of us pressed it, which was just as well because it saved us from having to get into some chest-bumping business ourselves. Clanging and banging in the alley alerted us the dump truck was coming and Rita had to stop, but she didn't really want to. Eyeing it warily, as if it were an auroch, she played until it got right up to us, then kicked the keyboard so hard it fell against the fence, and the only sound after that was my thundering heart.

Beth Spencer is an editor (Bear Star Press / www.bearstarpress. com) and writer who lives in rural Northern California with her husband and dog. Her book of poetry, *The Cloud Museum*, is available from Sixteen Rivers Press.

RECHARGEABLE MOONS

ARCHANA SRIDHAR

I stand under the street lamp on Spadina Avenue, staring up at the moon over the CN Tower, all lit up in red for the weekend's Santa Parade. The Beck Taxi pulls up and the driver greets me warmly.

"Archana—that sounds like an Indian name."

"Yes, my parents are from Bangalore. Where are you from?"

"Pakistan—Lahore." I wait for some unspecified tension to dissipate, but instead, "There's a game show on OMNI TV and the host is Archana Puran Singh. It is a beautiful name." We exchange further pleasantries, comparing our years in this country (me, nine, him, 35). We share an aversion to the cold ("joint pain") and a love of Niagara Falls ("the holiday lights are spectacular").

Then we fall into an easy silence for the long ride to the airport. Staring at the glass towers that have spread along Lakeshore Boulevard like the ice crystals along the car window, I suddenly miss my parents and I think he does too.

Out of nowhere, he says, "Have you heard about

that town in China that has its own moon? It charges itself by the sun. They don't even need streetlights anymore." I make a mental note to look that up, knowing I'll probably forget.

As he drops me off, he hauls my suitcase out of the trunk, sets it on the curb, and stretches his arms up to the sky, "In the future, Archana, maybe every town will have its own moon. Isn't that amazing?" And with that, he turns away, the fog of his breath dissolving into the frosty air as I wave from the sidewalk.

Later, seated at the Mill Street pub in Terminal 1, I scroll through my iPhone for information about the new moon over Chengdu. I learn that massive mirrors will soon unfurl across a tiny patch of space, redirecting the sun upon the glimmering Silk Road city each night, eight times as bright as the real moon. I drink my coffee and picture all of us transformed into a pearl necklace of spot-lit ant colonies under a celestial magnifying glass.

My gut twinges as I picture the babies of the future swaddled in nurseries halfway around the world, staring in wonder at fake moons and starry mobiles revolving overhead. Soon enough, those silver-foil satellites will cross gently in the night sky, leaving us without even the moon to share anymore.

Archana Sridhar is an Indian-American poet and university administrator living in Toronto. Archana focuses on themes of meditation, race, motherhood, and diaspora in her poetry and flash writing. Her work has been featured in *The Puritan*, *Jellyfish Review*, *Barren Magazine*, *The /tƐmz/ Review*, and elsewhere.

TEACUP WEREWOLF

JAN STINCHCOMB

Whatever you do, don't forget to feed the werewolf, Mom said before she died, or maybe it was before she left for Paris. We knew what she meant. He was the furry little creature who lived in our china closet, tucked into what happened to be my favorite teacup from our grandmother's set, which was hand-painted in a sentimental shade of pink with a gold edge. Mom said the werewolf gave us the blessing of perspective. He was so tiny it was easy for us to meet his needs, so old his bite could not transmit the dreaded infection. One of us would offer him a slender finger to gnaw on, and then a quick cauter-ization with a silver lighter would heal the wound. If he had been the usual size, Mom said, we would have been terrified and screaming on every full moon, trying to evade all that murderous manliness. Or manly murderousness. Or beastly drooling. He was cute and small and therefore our maternal hearts felt the need to nurture and protect him. Once, during an earthquake, I carried him outside in his teacup home. Family heirloom? a neighbor asked. You know it, I told her, treating the werewolf to three silver sprinkles, the kind the FDA warns you not to eat.

Sometimes, on hot evenings or long weekends, our husbands would threaten to get rid of him. Our laughter rang like silver bells. Where are you going to find a gun that small? Bullets that small? And don't forget: if you want to kill him, it takes a silver bullet to the heart, fired by the one he loves.

On cue my sisters and I would glance at each other, then down into the teacup, then over at the mirror, trying to catch a glimpse of true love or facial hair, whichever came first.

Jan Stinchcomb is the author of *The Kelping* (Unnerving) and *The Blood Trail* (Red Bird Chapbooks). She has been nominated for the Pushcart Prize, longlisted in the *Wigleaf* Top 50, and featured in *The Best Small Fictions 2018*. She lives in Southern California with her family.

MIKE TYSON RETROSPECTIVE

MATTHEW SUMPTER

Not iron: greased shoulders beneath industrial lamps of the Bellagio, his face leaning toward a microphone, promising Lennox Lewis, "I will kill your children. I want your heart."

*

I was a sick child—strep and allergies, gasping through my mouth as I waited for Afrin to drip like bitter metal down my throat.

*

I watched him: Tyson. He turned toward whatever sickness followed him around, and became it, biting off the edge of Holyfield's ear, sure, but then spitting it out, small and saliva-gemmed on the canvas. Blood pooled in his collarbone like a debt the world owed him for those years beneath the clouds of Brooklyn, father-less, unable to speak without a lisp.

*

Someone always pays, or should, though it fixes nothing.

*

I'm terrible at forgiveness. I have none for him or me or anyone I know. The past just hangs around like a broken stereo I can't turn off.

*

Years later, when I was finally well, a boy tackled me at recess. The wind flew out of my chest. My face crushed against the sleek swords of onion grass, and I swear I tasted pollen, ragweed, remembering those years breathless in a bed. I flipped the kid and choked him, longer than I should have, long enough for him to know.

Matthew Sumpter is the author of the poetry collection *Public Land* (Tampa Press, 2018). His individual poems have appeared in *The New Yorker*, *The New Republic*, *AGNI*, and *Poetry Daily*, and his short fiction has appeared in *Glimmer Train*. He is Visiting Assistant Professor of English at Tulane University.

THE BOAT PEOPLE

JEFF TAYLOR

All of my children have gone missing. I suspect the boat people next door, who are not refugees, but a bunch of miscellaneous ferals living in a vessel which is big and rotting on blocks. An abandoned project with flies spinning around the portholes and sacks for curtains.

I had about four, if I remember right. Or was it five? Their bedrooms echo like empty coffins, with small beds that have no-one left sleeping in them.

The Boat People squeeze evasive answers to my questions past their soggy roaches. The women have eye makeup as black as death and occasional teeth. Every one of them looks like a shell of the shell of their former lives. There's also this mangy dog that spends all day chowing down on what looks like a tumour on its paw.

My anxieties have started glowing like they just got new batteries.

Their leader has this one eye that's leaking bad, as if something in his head exploded, and a loser demeanour like he's always been the one without a chair when the music stops. I've been asked over to share their recreational habits, they have guest syringes, they said. But I might never get to come back.

I thought about reporting to the cops, but they're gonna want my children's names, and an exact number. My wife would likely know, but she's long gone off with what's-his-name.

There's a humming, and a vibrating, and a reeking, from that decaying boat in the prevailing wind. In the meantime I need some lines of communication, so I've decided to keep sending them messages in the empty bottles that I've drunk from.

Jeff Taylor is retired, and lives in Hamilton, New Zealand. He has had some success with short stories and flash fiction. He won the 2015 NZ Writers College Short Story and 2019 NZFF day competitions, and was awarded the 2016 Flash Frontier Summer Writing Award. His story, "The Boat People," was also nominated for the Pushcart Prize.

LADYBIRD

MARY THOMPSON

Let's say it's one of those rarer than rare days when the sun beams white out of a buttery sky. Let's say it's your first time with him and afterwards you drive over to the beach where you sunbathe and burn, then drag yourselves through the dunes to his white Cortina where he plays "Message in a Bottle" in his cassette player while you rest your feet on the dashboard and swig beer from a crate in the back. Let's say you spot a ladybird with two perfectly round dots inching its way slowly up the window and watch as he traces a line down the window onto your toes and up your thighs. Let's say you laugh as the ladybird follows the line down the window, onto the dashboard and inside your dress and you close your eyes as you feel the tickle of its minuscule legs. Let's say he kisses you and as he does so, you imagine how wonderful it would be to have that tiny, immaculate creature imprinted all over you.

And let's say you end up later in the Union Bar where it's dark, beery and rammed and you order a snakebite and black and drift past your friends, unaware.

"Oi," they shout. "Where've you been all day?"

"I honestly don't know," you say, and the boy by your side squeezes your hand and it feels so warm, so safe that you know this is exactly how it should feel. And let's say you order more of the purple stuff and drink it outside with him by the fountain in the park and the white sun streams through and the drinks glow crimson like a beautiful wound.

Mary Thompson works as an English tutor in London. She is a recent winner of two BIFFY 50 awards and has just been nominated for a Pushcart Prize. Her work has been published in various places including *Spelk*, *Ghost Parachute*, *Literary Orphans*, *New Flash Fiction Review*, *Pidgeonholes* and *MoonPark Review*.

BIRD WINGS

JENNIFER TODHUNTER

The first time I see her after surgery, her eyes are large like fried eggs. It bothers me, the way she stares unblinking, like she's watching a world I'm not privy to. *It's the morphine*, she says when I ask, then giggles.

She's been dyeing her hair for so long I have no idea when mine will go gray—but there are hints of it turning around her ears and at her temples. Things change so quickly when they're not looked after. She clutches shampoo and conditioner bottles in her hand while I help her shower, careful to avoid the bandages on her belly. Her weight loss is obvious now, the water pressure pushing her over. I reach out and steady her by the shoulder, the way she steadied me when I was younger, and am caught by how much her arm resembles the wing of a bird, its bones so intricate and light.

The doctor is trying to poison me, she says.

A man slips into my room every night, holding a knife with my blood on it, she says.

My husband, she starts. *My husband, my husband,*

my husband.

She's only been here four days.

Does she have any substance abuse issues? the doctor asks. *How much does she drink?*

The doctor doesn't ask why. Why she drinks so much, why she's so depressed, why she ignored her diverticulitis until it almost killed her.

My dad, I start, but cut myself off. The doctor isn't here to fix me.

At her house, the bottles in her kitchen cupboard are organized from largest to smallest, the way everything else in the space is organized. I tip the bottles down the sink, *glug, glug, glug*, until there's nothing left, and I haven't smelled anything so wretched since the shit-mix I made with girlfriends in ninth grade. Some of the bottles break when I drop them into the recycling bin, some don't. There are more bottles in the front hall cupboard. In the bathroom drawer. In the bedroom bedside table. I remove them all, just as the doctors removed part of her large intestine: methodically and carefully.

Back in her recovery room, I brush her hair, the way she used to brush mine; one hundred strokes a night.

Your hair is so soft, I say, *so pretty.*

She smiles at me, her ghastly oversized eyes trying

to catch mine.

Jennifer Todhunter's stories have appeared in *SmokeLong Quarterly*, *Necessary Fiction*, *CHEAP POP*, and elsewhere. Her work has been selected for Best Small Fictions and *Wigleaf*'s Top 50 Very Short Fictions. She is the Editor-in-Chief of *Pidgeonholes*. Find her at www.foxbane.ca or @JenTod_

THE QUIET OF GIRAFFES

CATHY ULRICH

In the paper the next morning, you read an article about a herd of giraffes they found in Central Africa that could speak.

Your wife is at the sink, washing dishes from last night's party, dries her hands on her apron front.

That can't be right, she says. *Giraffes can't speak.*

You rustle the paper, point at the article.

I mean, she says, *they don't have vocal cords.*

She says: *I read that somewhere. It's a fact.*

There is a bruise on the back of your wife's elbow where she can't see, from last night. Jim from three houses down, following her into the kitchen for another glass of wine and everyone running in after them when they heard the crash, your wife backed up against the counter, *he fell, he just fell*, wine spilled on the floor sticky beneath Jim from three houses down's head.

And everyone saying *Jim, hey, Jim, you okay?* and thinking what a shame it was his wife left and took the kids, down to Florida, they were saying, left him in that big house all alone, such a good guy, such a *great* guy, Jim from three houses down, and he sat himself up, rubbed his head, *I'm fine, I'm fine, I'm fine.*

You wouldn't let him leave till he could say how many fingers you were holding up and what year it was and his favorite joke, *I was talking to the duck,* and your wife smiling at the door beside you in her apron, and she fell asleep leaned up against you on the couch, watching the headlights of cars as they pulled out of your driveway, her left hand up around her throat, the soft sighs she exhaled, and she didn't move till morning, said, *oh, you should have woken me.*

Jim from three houses down will be found, finally, Wednesday afternoon, five days after your party, face down in his back yard, *subdural hematoma,* face gone purple from pooling of blood, no open casket for Jim, no trips to Florida to visit the kids, but your wife is asking you now *well does it at least tell you what the giraffes* said, and you read the article again and again to see, but no, it never does.

Cathy Ulrich is the founding editor of *Milk Candy Review*, a journal of flash fiction. She is the author of *Ghosts of You* (Okay Donkey Press), a collection of her Murdered Ladies flash. Her work has appeared in various journals and anthologies.

ANATOMICAL VENUS GIRL

CLIO VELENTZA

The class has moved on, but she stands transfixed in front of the glass case. The doll she's looking at could fit in her two hands. Its ivory parts have been carefully set aside: the coil of an intestine, a button-sized liver. A small heart, crown-shaped. The smooth lid of a bulging belly. The doll's eyes are closed, its face serene. A lovely, dead-saint's smile. The girl leans in, touches the inscription. Fifteenth century. So much time to spend undone, laid open.

The doll's hands rest over its hollow body, over the ivory figure of the curled up baby lying exposed inside her. The girl touches her own crown-shaped heart. She touches her own belly, looking for the same cold hollowness, the same exposed child. Hers is still hidden, so small it's barely there.

The doll's curls are loose over her lace pillow. The girl reaches up and tugs at her ponytail, and her hair falls around her shoulders. A museum guard walks by. *Excuse me*, the girl says. *Is nobody going to put her back together?*

Clio Velentza is a writer from Athens, Greece. She writes prose and plays, and her work has appeared in several literary journals and some anthologies. She is a winner of Best Small Fictions 2016 and *Wigleaf*'s Top 50 2019, and a Pushcart Prize and Best of the Net nominee.

WETS EATS WEST

EMILY F. WEBB

There was a cardboard sign and a thumb and everything else attached to the thumb was a cloud of green wool, gold sequins and red chiffon. The cardboard had only WEST written on it. The birds in the sky knew more about WEST than the vertical thumb attached to the arm held horizontally in the air. WEST was an abstract four-letter smile in his mind, but WEST was in the genetic wiring of a bird, the objective reality. If not WEST it would be STEW, or WETS, as long as it was not EATS. The boy and his arm and his thumb waited for two days before a purple Ford Fiesta picked him up and he sat in the car quietly for a long time on the loud hot stretch of road travelling in what seemed like no direction at all.

Emily F. Webb is the 2019 World Airsoft Champion.

BITE

CHARMAINE WILKERSON

Later, she would say that he had been blessed but first, she would curse the fleshy lip of the mushroom, sprouting there in the shade along the path where the boy walked daily, back and forth from the mines, his bare feet scuffing the red dirt, his fingernails seamed with mud. And it was the yearning, not the weight of the leaden sacks on his bony shoulders, not the hours spent picking through dusty pieces of rock in search of metal, that put him in harm's way on that day. Mineral dust took longer to scar a person's lungs, tainted water took time to grow a tumor. It was the walk home, an empty-bellied trek along a stony path, a shortcut past the cool, wooded corner where his temple twitched as he reached down to pluck at the mushroom, that single moment of daring, that put the boy's shins within striking distance of the snake's fangs. Later, she would say that her son had been saved by the serpent's head and herbs which she had ground up and charred and rubbed into razor cuts on his body. She would say that a boy, as small as he, might have suffered more than just the fever and the retching. She would wipe the dirt from his face and feed him a spoonful of fufu and tell him that one day, he would grow as tall and strong as an ebony tree and live like a king.

Charmaine Wilkerson's fiction has been published in various anthologies and literary magazines. Her novella *How to Make a Window Snake* won the Bath Novella-in-Flash Award and the UK's Saboteur Award for Best Novella. Originally from New York, she is currently based in Italy.

GRIEF IN MODERATION

DIANE WILLIAMS

A necessary and great object of interest—he had first found Valentina standing among other members of her family.

Her clothes were a deep purple to blue color and as her wet hair dried, it began beguilingly to curl.

And she was fragrant and Tom thought she was showy. She is not common in the wild.

And lots of other people still go up to her and consider her the way Tom does.

Most persistently, she brings into view a face that displays full-bodied welcome.

One weekday evening, in a local restaurant, a very tall drunk man walked over to the pair, kissed Valentina on the mouth, and then departed quickly.

Tom had questions. It was a puzzling capper to a typical day.

Tom, on that day at work, had closed out tax cases upon which no tax was due, and awaited a repairman to discuss the photocopier failure.

And Valentina has responsibility for all of the patients on her hospital shift, as well as the building, and people are responsive to her, sometimes fervently.

However, she did not respond to Tom's questions. She kept at her meat. She might otherwise have been caught in contradictions, but then she backed up in her chair and she gave her husband her answers: *But it isn't true. I don't recall. Sort of. Yes, I sometimes do.*

At bedtime Valentina lay on her back, arms at her sides, as did Tom—no intertwining and no tender touch that needed to become better still, except that their small-patterned wallpaper seemed to be excited the next morning.

The tiny daisies were scored by the shadows of the slats of the venetian blinds and the stripes were shivering.

And also at dawn, there was Valentina's instrumental smile! Her sign of sweetness that is the flying start, the fresh impetus, the feature on her face that creates her particular style.

And in theory she well understands any person's right to have privacy; to challenge and to complain without fear of reprisal; to make known his or her wishes; to receive complete information. To be wrenched.

Diane Williams is the author of nine books of fiction including her most recent—*The Collected Stories of Diane Williams* (Soho Press, 2018). Her stories appear frequently in *Harper's*, *London Review of Books*, *The Paris Review*, and *Granta*. She is also the founder and editor of the literary annual *NOON*.

LIMINAL

SHELBEY WINNINGHAM

lim·i·nal

/'limənl/

Adjective technical

adjective: **liminal**

1. relating to a transitional or initial stage of a process.

2. occupying a position at, or on both sides of, a boundary or threshold.

The waitress at the Waffle House definitely thought we were lovers. She greeted us with a seductive grin, like she was in on our little secret, and she didn't ask if we wanted to split the bill—she just brought us one ticket: one blueberry waffle, two orders of hash browns, a side of bacon. I noticed the two middle-aged men in the booth adjacent to ours staring at us over the brims of their coffee mugs; did they think we were lovers too? And what's more, were they repulsed at the thought, or were they a little turned on by it? That wasn't something I wanted to think about. Besides, I was too drunk, and it was too late for me to really think clearly. When my lover who was not my lover at all asked me if I was ready to go, I struggled to remember where we were. I could have been in any Waffle House in the world; they were all the same place after all. I imagined entering the Waffle House in Conway, Arkansas and exiting the Waffle House in Aurora, Colorado, just 463 miles from the Great Salt Lake Desert. When I awoke the next morning, sleep gluing my eyelashes together, her body so close to mine in the room we shared, the scent of vodka still filling up my nose, I mourned for all the girls who had ever loved her. Sometimes now, when I look in the mirror, I do not even recognize myself; I have changed so much I doubt you would recognize me either.

Shelbey Winningham is a senior Creative Writing major at Hendrix College in Conway, Arkansas where she lives with her cat. An Arkansas native, Shelbey has always harbored a love for literature. Her work has appeared in *Arkana*, *Underground*, *Bending Genres*, and other literary magazines.

QUANTUM PHYSICS ALLOWS FOR PARTICLES TO BE IN TWO STATES AT THE SAME TIME

JO WITHERS

I could tell you the load and force of every movement, how much energy it takes to climb, how much is expended on the descent. While I'm on the pole, I complete equations from memory, calculate the angle of my limbs and gravity's impact on my position. I dangle upside down with measured precision, seeming ethereal and weightless, watching as they gape below, waving their cash; the cause to my effect.

We're all the same here. The topless girl behind the bar studies English Literature at Oxford, sticks scribbled notes beneath the beer pumps so she can cram Chaucer between men. She wears her flame red hair braided down one side like Arthur's Guinevere. It whips round like an angry rattlesnake when she's on their laps. She has a feral fierceness, like some Viking warrior; she's the only one of us who hasn't called security in the private rooms. She's beautiful, but most nights she's off her face before the shift ends, sits sniffling on a stool, half the average weekly wage bulging from her thong. Sobs that she is Ibsen's Nora, pirouetting in the doll's house they've provided.

The new girl takes to centre stage in feathers. She's on a scholarship from Romania, her European drawl has the old guys piling in whenever she works the door. They ask her if she's Russian and she does the same blank smile every time and whispers that she can be anything they want her to be. She's a mathematical genius, can do long division to five decimal places in her head. She can calculate our rates by the second. Says on a busy night like tonight, we rake in twelve pence a second—better than any lawyer in the land.

I slide softly down the pole, balancing my mass delicately on one pivotal point. When I reach the bottom, I arch my back, hands and feet on polished floor, forming a perfect perpendicular triangle. I hold it, hearing their low whistles as they catch an eyeful; slow my breath and count to 20 while the money rolls in, wishing I could calculate how much would be enough.

Jo Withers writes short fiction for children and adults from her home in South Australia. Her recent work has featured in *The Caterpillar, Milk Candy Review, Ellipsis Zine, Bath Flash Fiction Anthology* and *Reflex Fiction*. Jo occasionally tweets @JoWithers2018

MIDNIGHT ON THE MOON

FRANCINE WITTE

is a lonely place, black as the end of hope, like a rocket that ran out of fuel and places to go. Like a man who, down on Earth, just swore undying love to his wife and sees his lover's face on the wall behind her.

The wife is a trusting thing, a planet hanging in the sky of his life, faithful and constant. She will always be there for me, he thinks. The man is happy, and the wife is happy, and, miles away, even the lover is happy.

Only the moon is lonely. Only the moon sees the truth. Even with the sun shining all day on its squinty eyes.

The man swears his love again. The wife believes him. And then, later, much, much later, in the white gauzy near-morning, he will enter her, like doubt.

MIDDLE OF NIGHT,

FRANCINE WITTE

too late for candy or games. Scratch of Mommy's slippers in the hall. We are three days without my father who left to who knows where? Came home from work like a night of storms and slammed his fist on the table. Saying words like "fired" and "bastard." Angry, like when he told Mommy he never wanted kids, and me, listening at the door. A terrible thing to never want your father back, but I'm thinking of tomorrow morning, breakfast of oranges, bacon curling into smiles, Mommy all to myself, and the cloud of my father in someone else's sky.

Francine Witte is the author of two flash fiction chapbooks, one full-length collection, *Dressed All Wrong for This* (Blue-light Press) and a novella-in-flash (Ad Hoc Fiction.) She lives in New York City.

A BRIEF PROGRESSION OF NATURAL DISASTERS

TARA ISABEL ZAMBRANO

AVALANCHE

When you insert your fingers inside me, I imagine the scar on your wrist, advancing like a crack in the windshield, cascading sticky junk out of me, its smell filling the room. I say your name out loud and you whisper, shh … we aren't young anymore.

VOLCANO

When you say you're still hungry and cut yourself while slicing an apple. I suck on your finger, a faucet now, your blood swimming in my veins, a lava-sheen sealing all the open spaces under my skin.

SINKHOLE

When the storm warning goes off and we sit together in the closet—an inch separating us. We talk about the towns we grew in, people we'd want to meet again; shake their hands and kiss their foreheads. As a middle-schooler, you followed the rail tracks across towns, over the swelling rivers, the markings like barbed wires on the maps—snaking, touching and leaving.

I count the towns where we've had sex. I think of the places I've had sex with someone else.

EARTHQUAKE

When the night is pale and noisy, we don't ask each other—Are you awake? We hear our breath, the creaking bed strings, the deep creases on the sheets like fault lines. We try to make shapes from our clothes hanging in the corner.

FLOOD

When you get up even though your sleeping pills and water bottle are on the side table next to the bed. I stir as if I was asleep, and you say the house walls are closing in on you. Outside, on the pavement, you look up at the star-throbbed sky and ask what day it is. We keep going around the neighborhood, trotting through the darkness until we are slick with dew.

TORNADO

When you come back and sit in the study, talk about the love letters we wrote to each other, the stickers we used, the way we signed our names. You say you miss writing letters. You say despite your best efforts there's a missed turn flagged on the road of our marriage. Your eyes gaze into mine as if you know about my screw ups. I suck the air and turn around to leave, my secrets flying like debris within the funnel of my body, my heart a rotating steam devil.

Tara Isabel Zambrano works as a semiconductor chip designer. Her work has been published in *Tin House Online*, *The Southampton Review*, *Slice*, *Triquarterly*, *Yemassee*, *Passages North*, and others. Recently she served as Flash Fiction Editor at *Newfound.org*. Tara moved from India to the United States two decades ago and holds an instrument rating for single engine aircraft. She lives in Texas.

THREE ESSAYS ON CRAFT

DISRUPTIVE DUALISM IN MICROFICTION, OR NIGHT SKY WITH STARS IN REVERSE

AIMEE PARKISON

Microfiction lends itself to the innovation of experiment and the compression of poetry. When it works, it moves us, often in ways so subtle and so sudden we don't realize what has happened until it's over. Brevity demands innovation. Brevity also demands that the writer immediately grab hold of the reader and never let go. Microfiction must take us on a journey in the shortest of time. That journey, though sudden, must provide the urgency and trans-formative quality we expect from longer travels.

Unlike traditional narratives, microfiction might not have all the basic elements deemed "necessary" for fiction. There might not be a fully defined narrative arc, character arc, conflict, rising action, falling action, climax, detailed setting, and reso-lution. However, microfiction may possess some, most, or all of these elements. Or not. More often, microfiction redefines fiction—writing basics through the innovation of compression by using a sort of implied narrative for world building. In this unconventional, compressed world building, the understory of innuendo, cultural context, artful subtext, and understated clues lure the reader into unspoken concerns at the heart of the story. What is unspoken drives the narrative, or rather the anti-narrative, of the short-short story.

In place of a traditional conflict, lurks a more subtle organic yet intangible tension. It creates a new sort of conflict where moods and images confront each other in dynamic opposition, creating moments of humor in the somber, moments of brightness in the shadow. Peppering brightness with sobering darkness, like a night sky with stars in reverse, it dazzles as it disorients.

Delicious tinges of insight, irony, and surprise are brought on by flashes of awakening in the formal relief that comes from the clashing of binary oppositions. Conflicting dichotomies reveal a spectrum of experience: brightness in darkness, humor in sadness, dignity in the downtrodden, ugliness in beauty, beauty in the face of ugliness, hope in despair, joy in depression, flashes of grief in happiness or sparks of happiness in the depths of grief, a sudden recognition of the familiar in the strange, horror lurking in the mundane, tenderness in violence, or violence in tenderness.

Disruptive dualism awaits at the heart of all art alive enough to awaken us to our sleeping selves. Sometimes dualism comes from humor, sometimes irony, but always a turn, a reversal, surprising yet necessary. When earned through the careful crafting of language and world building, transformative opposition in microfiction brings realistic and often shocking insight. This insight comes from the sort of questioning that ensues when something bleak is transformed by a moment of brightness or when something seemingly mundane is suddenly revealed as earth-shattering.

The narrative power of microfiction evolves from a sort of dichotomy disrupted when binary oppositions of mood, category, or image are broken by dualism. This dualism, once revealed, makes us question everything, exposing the irony of the human condition: creatures full of life, we live with the knowledge we must die. We are death and life combined. We are happiness and sadness, joy and terror, good and evil, male and female, old and young, violent and gentle, all in the same life. From the realistic to the most surreal of works, if fiction is functional, it gains power through the disruption of binary thinking, a questioning that invites awareness of the spectrum of complex emotions and experience at the heart of the human condition.

The best microfiction accomplishes this awakening of the gray matter's gray areas through its turns, turning on itself and sometimes against itself through irony—undercutting with verbal irony, surprising with situational irony, or unsettling with dramatic irony. Always, where there is darkness, there must be a hint of light, and where there is brightness, some shadow play. Without this tonal range of mood orchestration, tension and artistic effect are lost.

Like all good art, microfiction seduces us. It lures us into dreaming, into remembering the forgotten, into accepting the unacceptable, into admitting the shortfalls of our own private longings. It reminds us who we are, who we used to be. It does this by questioning what was, what might have been, what may be. It asks us questions and then refuses to answer. Always, the artistic gravitas lies in asking the right questions, in finding the right questions, never in offering or finding the right answers. Questions are valuable. Answers are not to be trusted.

Aimee Parkison is the author of *Girl Zoo*, *Refrigerated Music for a Gleaming Woman*, *Woman with Dark Horses*, *The Innocent Party*, and *The Petals of Your Eyes*. Parkison has won the FC2 Catherine Doctorow Innovative Fiction Prize, a Christopher Isherwood Fellowship, and the *North American Review* Kurt Vonnegut Fiction Prize. She teaches in the creative writing program at Oklahoma State University and serves on FC2's Boards of Directors.

Our staff editors asked Kathryn Kulpa, with 3 included stories in Best Microfiction 2020, to talk about her process.

PROMPTLY

KATHRYN KULPA

I confess: I write with prompts.

I've heard people speak of writing exercises dismissively: that they're too artificial, only good for beginners, not for "real" writers. Yet all my stories in this anthology, and almost all the stories I've written, grew out of prompts or exercises. Either a prompt got them started, or a writing exercise helped enrich a later draft. For me a good writing prompt—and it can be as simple as a picture or a list of words—is like playing scales before a concert or stretching before a run. A permission to begin.

"Why I Got Written Up by the Manager at Uncle Earl's World-Famous Bar-B-Q" was inspired by a restaurant menu: *boneless, smoky, honey-glazed*. The sensuality of the food descriptions brought me an image of the passionate, time-strapped servers, stealing hot kisses in the walk-in freezer. It also took me back to the world of low-wage service work. "No such thing as a smoke break!" was a saying of the manager at one of my old retail jobs, and I'm not sure I would have remembered it if the restaurant prompt didn't call up that world for me. The prompt didn't include a word limit, but I imposed one on myself, distilling everything down to that one guilty moment, so the tightness of the story reflected the urgency of the lovers.

"Warsaw Circus" came from a picture prompt: a circus photo of a woman dancing with a baggy-pants clown. I can't say I have good associations with clowns, generally. More terrifying than warm and fuzzy. But something about this picture captured me; the clown wasn't creepy, and I sensed a real tenderness between him and the woman. I'm not sure where the idea of a child hiding under his baggy costume came from, but once that image came to me, the story wrote itself. That sense of the circus as a liminal world, a world of border crossings, of sleight of hand. They are hiding in plain sight, deceiving with play. They are dancing with death.

A good writing prompt, for me, is one that's open-ended enough to allow freedom of expression, but offers just enough constraint to provide a challenge. Flash fiction, by definition, contains a constraint: brevity of form. For me it opens up the door to that liminal space in a way that a blank page does not.

Our staff editors asked Frankie McMillan, with 3 included stories in Best Microfiction 2020, to talk about her process.

THROWING OUT A LINE

FRANKIE MCMILLAN

I often write in bed. I think of it as my island, a little removed from the world. In my relaxed state images and surprising connections arise (horizontal position) followed by a swift resolve to begin tapping away on the laptop (sitting position). My other favourite writing place is in a studio I share with my artist daughter. It's set alongside other artist/theatre studios in a large overgrown orchard and was once the site of an alternative school. I've begun to associate the smell of paint and turps with the creative process.

Most of my stories are written in the one sitting. If I can't get something good out in that time I tend to move onto something new. A sitting can be anywhere between two to four hours. I often arrive downstairs about lunchtime, dishevelled and hungry and wondering where everyone has gone.

Once the story is down, I read it aloud as this alerts me to any clunkiness in language. Then I check 'for 'emotional truth.' This is where I get serious. Does the story reflect the complexity of the human condition or does it shed light on some new aspect of it? I want the words to matter. And I like what Kafka famously said. 'A book should be the axe for the frozen sea inside us.' I think to a large extent my stories exist before the writing process begins; they come from who I am ie a person who often finds others strange and can also be a stranger to herself.

In my story 'The Fish My Father Gave Me' I'm revisiting an old memory. My father, often absent, once came home with a chocolate fish for me. I knew the fish was for eating, not playing with in the bath but I persisted in making it 'swim'. Once I had the first line, 'I drowned the fish even though I was too old to be drowning a fish' I let myself be led by the story; allowing thoughts to snag onto each other, words to attract other words and connections to be made. Overall, I find it's best if I can 'get out of the way of myself' and let the writing come from feelings rather than carefully thought out ideas.

WHAT THE EDITORS SAY: INTERVIEWS WITH
THE YEAR'S TOP MICROFICTION MAGAZINES

CHRISTOPHER JAMES

JELLYFISH REVIEW

> *What do successful microfiction writers do to achieve empathetic character/s in just a page or two? How do they make us care in so few words?*

Excellent question! If you watch as many romantic comedies as I've watched, you'll know how films make the viewers care about their leads. The man goes to a market on a sunny day and buys an ice-cream for a little girl on crutches who's dropped hers. The woman dips her USB in her tea, losing the big project she's spent all week working on. Oh no! We let the films do this to us because we know we're going to spend a lot of time with the characters—we forgive the movie makers for taking shortcuts. But a microfiction writer doesn't have that luxury, so I think empathy comes from an awful lot of understanding *off* the page. The writer *knows* these characters, *loves* these characters, and the care *they* have for them shines right through and translates itself to us.

> *Do you see a surge of enthusiasm in the microfiction form?*

I think so. We're seeing more microfiction in our

submissions queue. But more than that, we've started seeing microfiction crop up in the bookstores over here in Jakarta. And if microfiction has made it to Jakarta, then it's very much already on the map!

What do you feel your magazine offers that is unique in the world of online literary journals?

When we started, we maybe offered a different kind of community experience, but now there are more places that do the same—that do it better than we ever could. So I think we have to keep working hard to provide something important and necessary. We try to bring the passions we hold dear to the work we publish. As long as we're doing something that still feels relevant and exciting to us, then I know we're doing okay. Also, and I can't stress this enough, we make more octopus puns than anybody else.

Can you offer a few tips for writing startling pieces that stand out?

Read, read, read, read, read. Everything else comes from there.

What are your goals for Jellyfish Review in the coming years?

We set ourselves annual targets. This year we want two thirds of the work we share to come from women writers. We want 40% of the work to be by writers of colour. We want to introduce more guest editors. We want to be in a position to pay, at least for special issues. And we want to publish less often, and find other ways to maintain a fast momentum.

Would you recommend any microfiction to people interested in the form?

One of the most striking pieces I read in the last couple of years was "The Doll's Alphabet," by Camilla Grudova. It's two lines long, and I have no idea what it means, and I'm obsessed with it. An amazing work.

KIM MAGOWAN

PITHEAD CHAPEL

What do successful microfiction writers do to achieve empathetic character/s in just a page or two? How do they make us care in so few words?

Micro relies on many tools of poetry. When I reread the four stories selected for *Best Microfiction 2020*, I note each story uses startling, distinctive imagery. That imagery captures, in a compressed space, how the I (and the eye) of each story sees the world. For instance, Jennifer Todhunter's piercing "Bird Wings" opens with the narrator describing her mother's eyes: "The first time I see her after surgery, her eyes are large like fried eggs. It bothers me, the way she stares unblinking, like she's watching a world I'm not privy to." We immediately know that the narrator's mother is drugged and disoriented, via her eyes like "fried eggs." But also, interestingly, we watch the narrator watch her mother watching, and we see the narrator observe her own exclusion. A complex voyeurism is at play. In Michelle Ross's story "Fertilizer," the narrator makes a similar sharp, precise observation: "I don't remember what we watched, but I remember it was winter, the scratchy nubs of grass on his lawn frosted over." When we editors first encountered this story in the queue, we were all immediately taken by those distinctive "scratchy nubs": Ross economically depicts a lawn that instead of being fertile is cold, sharp to the touch, brutalized, exhausted. The images in these four stories work almost like verbs. They perform a lot of essential, extremely compact action.

Are there subjects you›d like to see more of?

I would love to see more bizarre new worlds, like the one Kyra Kondis paints in "The Day the Birds Came," where "we," the first person plural narrators, watch their classmate Patricia get mysteriously stalked by birds. This story is delightful yet menacing, depicting a world that is both familiar and strange. Part of what is strange is that instead of being aghast or concerned that Patricia has been entirely subsumed by birds— "And then, there was no more Patricia—there were just birds" —her classmates are envious, longing: "we doodled wings on our math homework. *She's so lucky, she's so interesting, she's so cool.*" Are the birds an analogy for boys, whose attention at a certain age feels both desirable and oppressive? What exactly does the story mean? I like that I don't know, that it leaves me wondering. I want more oddball mysteries.

Do you see a surge of enthusiasm in the microfiction form?

Absolutely! I see that surge of enthusiasm in my Submittable queue at *Pithead Chapel*, as we get increasing numbers of flashes and micros, I see it in my Twitter feed, I see it among my students at Mills College. Micro is having its day in the sun. I don't know exactly how to account for this, but I vociferously dispute one (dumb) theory I've heard, that micro is popular because our attention spans are shorter. Nothing could be farther than the truth! Micro, like poetry, demands alert, sharply attentive readers. Micro insists upon real concentration. I suspect the reason for micro's current popularity has to do with the craft it requires. I've noticed that once writers try micro and flash, they quickly get addicted to the form. In my own experience, paring stories to the bone has made me a better writer, because it forces me to pay attention to every word. The skills reading and writing it requires are portable: we carry them to longer work.

What do you feel your magazine offers that is unique in the world of online literary journals?

Before I became Fiction Editor for *Pithead Chapel*, I was a writer submitting stories to them. The thing that first caught my attention about *Pithead Chapel* was this description in the mission statement: "Most of all, we want your work to make us feel something ... We want your work to leave a brilliant bruise." I love that image of the "brilliant bruise." That pretty pain is what I'm looking for in fiction as a reader, and what I'm aiming for as a writer: I want stories to punch. At *Pithead Chapel*, we are dedicated to publishing and promoting both new and established writers. In my almost two years there, we've published some of my all-time idols (my jaw dropping as I saw particular names in the queue), and we've also been the very first publication of one wonderful writer. Both finds thrill me. Our goal is to publish, perfect, and promote the strongest work possible, with the larger goal of strengthening the writing community we are all part of.

Can you offer a few tips for writing startling pieces that stand out?

The key thing with micro is there is no room for flab. You must start strong: look at the opening lines of our four stories. They warp-speed the reader into the story's specific world. Micros are all about the perfect detail that communicates efficiently and precisely what you most need to know. Note how in "Mike Tyson Retrospective," Matthew Sumpter describes Mike Tyson "biting off the edge of Holyfield's ear, sure, but then spitting it out, small and saliva-gemmed on the canvas." That wonderful compound adjective, "saliva-gemmed," turns something grotesque into something oddly transformed, almost beautiful. Finally, the shorter a story is, the more crucial the ending. My friend Grant Faulkner, editor of *100 Word Story*, likens the last line of a micro to the end of a gymnastics routine: you've got to stick the landing.

MARY LYNN REED &
LESLEY C. WESTON

MOONPARK REVIEW

> *What do successful microfiction writers do to
> achieve empathetic character/s in just a page or two?*

We think one of the keys to writing empathetic
characters is to immerse the reader in the world of
the story completely. For micros it's crucial that
this immersion occur swiftly, without hesitation or
resistance. That is true for both of the *MoonPark*
micros featured in your 2020 volume. Within the
first few sentences we feel the beating heart of the
character and the tension of their world.

> *Are there subjects at MoonPark Review you'd
> like to see more of?*

We don't have any particular subjects we favor.
What attracts us to new work, on any subject, is a
unique perspective, and a strong image. We are a
journal of short prose, and the thing we would like
to see more of are hybrids (e.g., in forms like haibun).

> *What do you feel your magazine offers that is
> unique in the world of online literary journals?*

First, there are many great online literary journals

operating today that we admire so we aren't sure that anything we're doing is completely unique but here are some things we are proud of:

We are a two-person editorial team with no additional readers. Every story submitted is read in its entirety by an editor. And every story published is agreed upon by both editors. Over time we feel like this has created a unique editorial aesthetic for *MoonPark Review* that captures the best of both of our editors' viewpoints.

We are also proud of the simple, clean aesthetic of our web-based publication (with no clutter or advertising), and for every piece we publish we produce an original illustration, inspired by the story or prose poem. This illustration is also a collaboration of the two editors, one as artist, the other as "gentle critic and final-approver."

We are proud to be a fast-response market (with a five-day average response rate), we are always open for submissions, and there is no submission fee.

Can you offer a few tips for writing startling pieces that stand out?

Instead of following tips or prompts, we'd rather writers found their own unique voice. Tell your startling stories in the way only you can.

You have been publishing flash and microfiction for quite a while. Anything you›d like to say about how the form is evolving and changing over the years?

The main change we see in our queue is the ascendancy of the micro form. Our maximum word count is 750 but the majority of the work we receive is less than 300 words. And we believe our strongest published work is in the micro range. We also love the prose poem and are pleased to be seeing, and publishing, more of them.

MoonPark Review publishes 13 pieces (or writers) every quarter. Do you see that changing in the future?

No. We like our quarterly publication schedule and we love the number 13. We've found that this pace allows us to give the proper attention to every piece we publish: creating the illustrations, providing proofs for writers to review before publication, and promoting the issues and our authors on social media.

ROBERT JAMES RUSSELL

CHEAP POP

What do successful microfiction writers do to achieve empathetic character/s and relatable stories in just a page or two?

It's a combination of things, but there is a noticeable difference in successful flash fiction pieces when the author has given considerable thought to the characters' backstories *before* they write and/or understands what they hope to accomplish with the piece (and have some idea of *how* and *why*). Vignettes, especially, work—and work well—when it isn't thought about in a vacuum, an "Oh, that'd be neat" mentality. Even for the most isolated scenario on the page, authors should know *why they're writing this scene*—why it exists and what they want to do with it. A frequent mistake I see with early writers is to confuse details with complexity; adding detail just to add detail, especially in a truncated space, will serve to muddle the meaning and/or make the characters seem wholly created, as opposed to *real* and, therefore, empathetic. We want these microspaces to be confessionals—we want to be invited into their lives and feel the totality of their existence, even if we only get a tiny bit of that on the actual page. I honestly think *relatable* can be applied to any situation or environment, any profession or background, no matter how idiosyncratic or uncommon; even in a piece without a strong presence of a character (focusing more on the *place* than the people in it), a writer who has thought about *why here* and *why this* will succeed in giving us so much to think about and be entirely relatable.

Are there subjects you'd like to see more of in your submissions?

CHEAP POP looks for the totality of human existence. If it's done well, it's done well. I do think quiet moments can end up being so cathartic and affecting in small spaces, as opposed to trying to cram in too much too fast. Show me your ride on the bus, the cold walk home, the newly-frozen-over landscape you pass, the quiet dinner out at the restaurant, or sitting in front of a fire contemplating the ways in which you interacted with the world (or ways in which you wish you had). That innerspace, I find, is just wonderfully fertile for microfiction. So, short answer: I'm game for anything.

Which microfiction writers do you enjoy reading on a fairly regular basis?

Ah! Too many. So, instead of a list, I'll say, very

sincerely: I'm inspired by every piece and person we publish at *CHEAP POP*. And the folks selected for the *Best Microfiction 2020* anthology, too—these are the people I'm reading and re-reading, that are making me want to be a better writer.

What do you feel your magazine offers that is unique in the world of online literary journals?

I think one of our greatest virtues is how we cap our word count at 500. It forces a concision that serves the work. If you can tell a story, make me feel, build a world in 500 words, that's masterful. That draws people in. That makes people stop—if only for a moment—to inhabit the space. Readers know that's what they're in for when they click on one of our links; writers welcome the craft challenge. We've also been around for a while! I feel so fortunate at the sheer amount of quality flash fiction we've been able to publish since we started in 2014. I feel very lucky that people seek *CHEAP POP* out, and however our reputation developed, I'm honored to help shepherd it all along.

Can you offer a few tips for writing startling pieces that stand out?

Be yourself. I don't care if you're a high school student or a 60-year-old writing your first piece:

don't write what you think we want to see. Write what you want, be true to your voice, and lean into it. It is abundantly clear in 2020, I think—and if not, I'll continue helping to make it so! —that the writing world today is a wonderfully new, vibrantly diverse place. We don't want writers to write to please us. We want true, human experiences, across the spectrum. We want to see, no matter how small, what makes you tick. What stands out, ultimately, is the *humanity* behind the human condition. The little bits and pieces that make your experience of the world unique are what makes your writing unique, too—how you view the world, how you move through it, is so wonderfully, idiosyncratically beautiful and I hope writers continue leaning into that, no matter what they're writing about. To me, that's how you stand out.

ZOE MEAGER

TAKAHĒ

What do successful microfiction writers do to achieve empathetic character/s and relatable stories in just a page or two?

I think quite often they forgo modern etiquette. While novels introduce characters with thoughtful details ("Reader, this is Character. Character has brown eyes and trouble buttoning her shirts"), shorter forms are more likely to plunge straight into "Wait till you hear this! Character's marriage is falling apart!" Just as people say that very short fiction has to start in the middle of the story, rather than the beginning, perhaps we should start in the middle of the character too.

Are there subjects you'd like to see more of in your submissions?

I love the way poets respond to current events and politics, it adds such energy, and it's exciting when we see it in short prose forms, too. Think of the hit that was Kathy Fish's "Collective Nouns for Humans in the Wild." Sometimes writers might worry that letting in the so-called real world will date their work, but short fiction has the advantage of an immediacy that's almost out of reach of longer prose forms, so exploit it, I say.

How have you seen your magazine grow and change over the years?

I started fiction editing for *takahē* at the start of 2019 and immediately broadened our submissions guidelines to allow for more very short fiction. I was over the moon to publish Frankie McMillan and Allan Drew—two of our Guest Fiction writers who gave us several short pieces instead of one longer story.

We also now have a special focus for print issues of publishing three or four short pieces from the same writer, which creates a real showcase of work and lets the pieces bounce off each other—the sets we published by Melanie Dixon and Rachel J Fenton were particular favourites.

It's a very exciting time in the New Zealand writing scene for flash and microfiction! Have you seen an increase in submissions, and in reader interest?

We've seen a huge increase in submissions, with lots more writers submitting very short pieces. *takahē* readers tend to be curious about what new writers have to say, and we've had an excellent response to the breadth of voices and styles.

Can you offer a few tips for writing startling pieces that stand out?

Well, there's that earlier business about etiquette. Another thing that strikes me when reading submissions is when a story's been hacked away at to its detriment, so I'd say be ruthless in editing your work, but don't be dictated to by word count. If you edit a story down to fit a submission opportunity and it's stronger for it, great. If not, you're much better off holding onto the longer version and waiting for the right submission opportunity to come along.

Can you turn us on to any other short form writers we may not know about yet (living or late)?

At the moment I'm getting so much out of Margarita Karapanou (1946–2008). The entire first chapter of her 1976 novel *Kassandra and the Wolf* is:

I was born at dusk, hour of the wolf, July, under the sign of Cancer.

When they brought me to her, she turned her face to the wall.

CATHY ULRICH

MILK CANDY REVIEW
AUTHOR, *THE QUIET OF GIRAFFES* (TINY MOLECULES)

As both a writer and editor of the form, can you offer other writers a few unusual writing tips?

I'm terrible at giving tips because my own writing process is such an instinctual thing. I don't sit down and think, "okay, how do I make this work, what do I do here." For me, I guess what's worked best is to let the words carry me to their destination.

That's not very helpful, is it! How's this? A writing tip I see get a lot of flak is "write what you know" because people think it means that they can't write outside of their own experiences, their own worlds. And I don't think that's what it should mean at all— it should mean write the stories you want: towering epics, fantasies, dramas, whatever. But use what you *know* to make it all feel real.

What do successful microfiction writers do to achieve empathetic character/s in just a page or two?

They don't skimp on detail or rely on stereotypes. I remember seeing a writer, when confronted by readers complaining about the use of stereotypes in a flash he'd written, say he had no choice *but* to use stereotypes because there's not enough room for development in flash. Which is ridiculous, of course, and lazy writing.

What the best micro writers are doing is creating snapshots of real, believable, *living* characters. They give the reader something real and true to connect to. All the best micro writers do it, present their readers with a version of the truth, something to believe in, something to cling to. Even in our tiniest pieces in *Milk Candy*, our writers always give the reader specific detail that anchors the piece.

What do you feel your magazine offers that is unique in the world of online literary journals?

There are so many amazing journals publishing amazing stories—I love that flash and microfiction are getting such wonderful representation. There are so many champions of the micro form nowadays, it's a great time to be reading and writing it.

What makes *Milk Candy* unique amongst all these wonderful publications is our tone, I think. Even our saddest stories carry a bit of hope, a bit of light. That tiny spark of light, that's really important to me for what *Milk Candy* represents.

Are there subjects that you›d like to see more stories written about?

You know, I'm not sure that there are. As long as

people are writing the stories that only *they* can tell, I'm satisfied with whatever subject they choose. What I like is a writer's unique perspective on a subject—this last year, I read a lot of school shooting stories. It's a horrible, horrible thing to have to write about, but at the same time it's something we *need* to be writing about. The ones that were strongest for me were the ones that *only* that author could have written. *That's* what I'd like to see more of!

> *You're a relatively new journal, and you are publishing the best microfiction out there! What a cool success story. Do you have suggestions for editors/publishers of literary journals just starting out?*

I'm so grateful to all of our contributors. I have been amazingly lucky to publish such powerful pieces from such powerful writers.

My suggestions for new editors/publishers would be to love what you are publishing and be supportive of your contributors. Every single story we've published is a story I personally love, and that makes it such a delight to share them. I really can't say enough how lucky I have been to work with amazing talents like *Milk Candy*'s writers.

BEST MICROFICTION THANKS THE JOURNALS WHERE THESE PIECES APPEARED IN 2019.

ALL MATERIAL USED BY PERMISSION.

"Why I Got Written Up by the Manager at Uncle Earl's World Famous Bar-B-Q" by Kathryn Kulpa and "Stained Lips" by Jan Elman Stout from *100 Word Story*.

"Wets Eats West" by Emily F. Webb from *The A3 Review*.

"This Is A Comb" by Leila Ortiz from *Anomaly*.

"Teeth" by Tim Fitts from *Apple Valley Review*.

"Liminal" by Shelbey Winningham from *Arkana*.

"The Fish My Father Gave Me" by Frankie McMillan and "The Kitchen" by Curtis Smith from *Atticus Review*.

"Giants" by Steven John and "Palate Cleanser" by Michelle Ross from *Bending Genres*.

"Historic Preservation" by Kathryn Kulpa from *Cabinet of Heed*.

"Fable Told from the Future West" by Austin Sanchez-Moran and "We Dive" by Sarah Freligh from *Cease, Cows*.

"Weight Room" by Paul Crenshaw, "Men's Secrets"

by Lenora Desar, "Still Life with Prairie, 1860" by Natalie Teal McAllister, "Brass" by Melissa Ostrom, and "Toddy's Got Lice Again" by Tucker Leighty-Phillips from *CHEAP POP*.

"Ted Cruz Attends a Goldfish Funeral" by E. Kristin Anderson and "Her Wing" by Catherine Edmunds from *Cherry Tree: A National Literary Journal at Washington College*.

"The Horses Are Ready and They Need to Go" by Christopher Citro and "Compensation" by Ken Poyner from *Cincinnati Review*.

"Here Are The Things The Moon Told Me During The Lunar Eclipse of January 21, 2019" by Ashely Adams from *Cotton Xenomorph*.

"Exit Music" by Beth Ann Spencer from *Flash Flood*.

"How to Tell a Story from the Heart in Proper Time" by Riham Adly and "Bloom" by Kari Nguyen from *Flash Frontier*.

"Down the Long, Long Line" by Mary-Jane Holmes from *FlashBack Fiction*.

"Doc Holiday Goes West" by Aleyna Rentz from *Flock*.

"Why I Love Penguins" by MFC Feeley from *Ghost Parachute*.

"Grief In Moderation" by Diane Williams, as first appeared in *Granta Magazine*, September 23, 2019.

"One day an orgasm decides to move to Spain" by

Nin Andrews from *hashtagart.com magazine*.

"the summer heat feels just like love" by JJ Peña from *Into the Void*.

"When You First Meet the Telepath" by Meghan Phillips, "Rechargeable Moons" by Archana Sridhar, and "A brief progression of natural disasters" by Tara Isabel Zambrano from *Jellyfish Review*.

"The Grand Am" by Tyler Barton from *JMWW*.

"Ponds" by Pamela Painter and "Escape Into the Waking World" by Mary Grimm from *The Journal of Compressed Creative Arts*.

"An inventory of the possessions of William Kevin Thompson, Jr., age 19, upon his expulsion from the family residence on October 20, 1971" by Thaddeus Gunn from *Kenyon Review Online*.

"Bite" by Charmaine Wilkerson from *Litro*.

"She Will Become a Bird Scientist" by Jenny Ferguson from *matchbook*.

"Flat Stanley grabs a burrito" by Jennifer Howard from *Maudlin House*.

"Sumo Wrestlers' Heating Service" by Robert Scotellaro from *Meniscus*.

"Warsaw Circus" by Kathryn Kulpa, "Anatomical Venus Girl" by Clio Velentza, and "Midnight on the Moon" by Francine Witte from *Milk Candy Review*.

"An Imaginary Number" by Sian Griffiths from *Monkeybicycle*.

"The Jumper" by Sarah Layden, "Dissolve" by Santino Prinzi, and "Cubism" by Daryl Scroggins from *MoonPark Review*.

"For Two Blue Lines" by Hema Nataraju from *MORIA Literary Magazine*.

"The Boat People" by Jeff Taylor from *National Flash Fiction Day NZ*.

"Lafayette Indiana" by Sarah Green from *New South Journal*.

"From the Slumbarave Hotel on Broadway" by Jules Archer and "Here" by Tommy Dean from *New World Writing*.

"A Quick Word About My Life" by Trent England from *Okay Donkey*.

"Kiss Me, Kiss Me, Kiss Me (1987)" by Josh Jones from *Paper Darts*.

"The Thing" by Collette Arrand from *Passages North*.

"The Day the Birds Came" by Kyra Kondis, "Fertilizer" by Michelle Ross, "Mike Tyson Retrospective" by Matthew Sumpter, and "Bird Wings" by Jennifer Todhunter from *Pithead Chapel*.

"Middle of Night" by Francine Witte from *Porter House Review*.

"Still Warm" by K M Elkes and "Heartwood" by Johanna Robinson from *Reflex Fiction*.

"Alice in Neverland" by Kyle Hemmings from *Sonic Boom*.

"Hit Man in Retirement" by Robert Scotellaro, "Ladybird" by Mary Thompson, and "Quantum Physics Allows for Particles to Be in Two States at the Same Time" by Jo Withers from *Spelk*.

"Sick Day" by Scott Garson from *Split Lip*.

"Swans May Bite Without Warning" by Melanie Dixon, "Dirty Mouth" by Frankie McMillan, and "The Story Inside Her" by Frankie McMillan from *takahē magazine*.

"The Book of X: Vision #13 (Throat Fields)" by Sarah Rose Etter from *The Adroit Journal*, excerpted from the novel, *The Book of X*, published by Two Dollar Radio.

"Caught" by CC Russell from *The Sonder Review*.

"Muscle" by Karen Smyte from *The Southampton Review*.

"How My Parents, Who Gave Me Up for Adoption, Might Have Met" by Epiphany Ferrell from *Third Point Press*.

"The Quiet of Giraffes" by Cathy Ulrich from *Tiny Molecules*.

"Skyscraper Woman" by Emma Hutton and "In my dream I see my son" by Jason Jackson from *TSS*.

"Just to Say" by Nathan Alling Long from *Vestal Review*.

"Settled" by Alice Maglio and "Teacup Werewolf" by Jan Stinchcomb from *Wigleaf*.